TOO DARK TO SEE

Chloë Heuch

Firefly

First published in 2020
by Firefly Press
25 Gabalfa Road, Llandaff North, Cardiff, CF14 2JJ
www.fireflypress.co.uk

A CIP catalogue record of this book is available from
the British Library.

ISBN 9781913102166
ebook ISBN 9781913102173

This book has been published with the support of
the Welsh Books Council.

Typeset by Elaine Sharples

Printed and bound by CPI Group UK

I would like to dedicate this book to my mum, Val. Thank you for books and tenderness, for my wide-open sky and the green patchwork of running. Thank you for home. This is for you.

CHAPTER ONE
AUTUMN

'That's Blackmoss.' Dad slows the car to a halt, as a mountain, speckled with boulders, rears up at the end of the lane. 'Last stop before the moors start, Kay. It'll be a great place to live. Think of all the walks we can go on. You can even get to Hagger Tor from here.'

Dad smiles at Mum, then turns in the driver's seat and gives me a big full grin, touched with desperation. I am hunched in the back seat, cheek resting on my fist. I check Mum's reflection in the wing mirror, but she stares blankly out, her face pasty and moon-shaped since the latest chemo.

'When I was a girl, I used to spend my summers up by Hagger Tor. There's a river at the bottom and we used to make dams,' she says to no one in particular.

Dad clears his throat, giving himself a moment to

think of something to say, something full of bright enthusiasm, something fake.

It happens in slow motion: first the sound of an engine barking; Mum and Dad's heads turn as one towards the sound; a battered old khaki Land Rover roars into view from Hagg Farm. There is a loud *CRACKKK* and Mum's reflection in the wing mirror is gone.

I lean forward to see the snapped wing mirror hanging loose from its wires like a broken neck, its single eye blinking as it swings.

Dad shouts, 'Bloody idiot!'

He bullets from his seat, leaving the driver's door open wide. He chases the Land Rover and bangs his fist on the window.

A short, fat man gets out, his finger in Dad's face, yelling about 'private property and no fucking right parking there.'

Dad says, 'You've no right to drive off when you've hit someone.'

Mum would usually be out there by now too, by his side, but she watches them through her milk-blue eyes, listless.

I climb out and hang onto the door, wanting to help Dad but afraid. The wind is gripping and cold, rattling under my jumper, up my sleeves, along my spine. I want Dad to let it go. As usual, he is doing his long-arm-of-the-law stuff.

The fat man is a barrel of anger. He lifts his arms up, his jacket rising and exposing a pale, fleshy stomach hanging over his belt. He pushes a finger into Dad's chest.

Dad takes a step away, his palms upward as he reasons.

'Dad!' I call. He either ignores me, or the wind steals my words.

The passenger door of the Land Rover opens. Someone steps out. Not a boy; he has a man's jaw, the clean precipice of weather-tanned skin. His buttery-brown hair is thick in the wind. Keeping his gaze down, he lopes round the vehicle, which is still farting exhaust fumes, and stands between the two adults.

He holds his arm to his face, a strong, sinewy arm, then he puts a hand on the farmer's sleeve. He speaks, but I can't hear him.

'Don't fucking tell me what to do!'

The fury has a new target. The lad flinches, but too late. The man swings out, and the loose fist lands on the lad's cheek. I see him stagger.

Dad steps forward to help him, but the lad dips away fast, his body shrinking into the Land Rover, cheek flushed.

Before he gets into the car, he looks at me, straight at me. His dark, long lashes frame the shame in his eyes. I duck slightly behind the door frame, but don't break the contact. All that is hurting and beautiful in that face burns itself into the backs of my eyes.

The farmer, fury spent, clambers into the driver's seat and is off even before his door slams shut.

'Hey!' Dad knocks on the window as they pass. 'You can't – that's assault…'

But they're gone.

Dad scratches his thinning temple. I know he is memorising the number plate, to log it when he next gets to work. He looks over the damage to our car, secures the broken mirror, then gets in, belting up, of course; always the copper.

'Some people…' Dad shakes his head in disbelief. 'That poor lad.'

His happy optimism moments ago is broken. The wind whistles through my half-closed window, and ripples the heather around us.

The thudding in my chest seems to ricochet around the car.

'Mum? Did you see that?'

But she doesn't reply. I lean forward between the seats. She has her eyes closed again.

'Will you report him, Dad?'

'Too right.' He grips the wheel and moves off cautiously. As the car trundles down the lane, Dad is quiet, his jaw set.

We pass the row of terraced houses once more. The one with the 'For Sale' sign, the one we came to view, has an empty, cold look. White clouds speed, high, high above us, the sunlight glinting and stony. No one speaks.

The hard knot in my stomach begins to melt as we turn out of the village. I sigh with relief. We are with the other traffic on the main road, the other normal people doing Saturday things. Going home.

That night, snug in bed, my head is still full of the rise of the mountain and the cold house; the punch, the reel and sway of the lad, the mute call for help in his eyes. Dad will do something. Dad will sort it. Mum will be back to normal soon and will get back to work. We will never need to move anyway.

I feel the safe distance between there and here as I drift to sleep, a distance I hope I will never have to cross.

CHAPTER TWO
WINTER

The funeral car seats are slippery. I keep having the urge to skid off them and make a joke, but no one is looking. We are driving to the church behind the hearse with the coffin in it. No one thought about it, but I don't have anything black to wear, so I have on my blue school trousers. I found an old black jumper, but it is ancient and has bibbles of fluff all over it.

As we walk from the car to the church entrance, a bus changes gear at the brow of the hill, slowing down. I glance up. It is full of younger pupils from my school. They watch, bored, inquisitive, some laughing. I feel so far away from them, like I've turned into an alien.

Dad pats my shoulder to make me move on. We walk down the church to the front. There are so many people, so many eyes. I want to look for Anna. I watch the back of my dad, until we are sitting facing the front, facing the coffin.

The reverend says lots of nice things. I am expecting I will cry, it is my Mum's funeral after all. But I don't. There are too many words, too many people, so I concentrate on my trousers. I had to iron them myself this morning and there are silvery sheens along the seams. I can see the cross-weave where the machine has knitted the material together. I concentrate on the minute black squares between the dark-blue criss of the material.

I have to remember to breathe. The coffin is right in front of me, with flowers. I am on the front row. The man at the altar is in the corner of my eye. I cannot look at him. I am facing the front, facing the front.

I hold Dad's hand. It is cold. He holds mine tight. With his other hand, he pulls a tissue from his pocket, and without making any noise, lifts it to his eyes. I wonder why the tears don't come for me. I ball up my fist and cut semi-circles with my nails into my skin.

After the funeral, everyone comes to our house and it is the most stupid, pointless event of the whole day. Mum's friends looking weepy; Aunt Theresa and her husband; our neighbours; people I don't even know, from Mum's work perhaps; loads of people squashed into our house, saying, 'Sorry, Kay, sorry.' There is food in the kitchen no one is eating. I sit on the stairs. Dad rushes past, his hair fluffed up. His eyes are flitting from one person to the next. I am going to cry.

I go into the toilet and lock the door. Theresa, my dad's sister, knocks and asks if I am all right. I say, 'Yes,' and press the flush. Even here I can't get away. Waiting outside, she hugs me, a lukewarm, just-for-show hug, holding her body away. I want to yell in her face, 'PISS OFF AND LEAVE ME ALONE.'

But I don't. I am buffeted by one conversation after another, humiliated by all the pitying eyes.

Anna, my best friend, arrives at last, cocooned in between her mum and dad. She looks washed and brushed. I feel tatty and neglected in my badly ironed clothes. She's got new earrings. She hugs me, and I squeeze her back.

'Kay,' Anna's mum says. More hugs, but these are different, remind me too much of what's gone. I pull away and my eyes trick me, flooding over only when I am trying so hard to stop them.

'Loving your new lobes!' I turn to Anna, flicking the silver tassels that delicately hang down from her ears.

'Thanks.' She smiles at me, but it's not her normal smile. She searches my face. I don't know what she is looking for. Her mum and dad move toward the dining room to collect a drink. Anna peels away from them. 'How you doing?'

'God, I am glad to see you. Dad is doing my head in, and if I have to spend any more time with the clean-freak I am going to explode!' I roll my eyes in Theresa's direction.

We automatically head up to my room. We pass Mum and Dad's bedroom door, the place where she died only eight days ago.

'I now know why Theresa never had kids. She'd have scrubbed them out of existence. It's all she does all day.' I flop onto my bed. 'I wish she'd go home.'

Anna smirks, but it is more out of politeness than genuine. She sits at the end of the bed and picks up the velvet cushion I got at Christmas, the one with the birds on. She seems far away. 'How much longer is she staying?'

I shrug. 'Day after tomorrow, I think. Then things might get back to normal.' Heat flushes my face. Normal. I feel self-conscious, as though I have to think what to say next.

'Are you coming back to school?' Anna strokes the velvet smooth.

9

'I didn't want to stay off. They made me. I can't believe I missed the Chemistry exam.'

'It was awful.' Anna makes a face. 'You can do it in the summer. I'll probably be re-sitting it with you.'

I throw a soft bear at her, but she doesn't throw it back. I don't want to think about school. Or exams. I get up and stare out of the window at the grey, damp street.

'Will you come for a walk?' I ask.

At the bottom of the stairs, she whispers something to her mum. I see Dad in the lounge. His shirt has got untucked at the back. I need to get out of here. I open the door, not knowing if Anna is coming or not. The cold is clammy on my skin.

'Don't you want a coat?' Anna asks, zipping up and snuggling into her hood.

'I'm OK.'

There are cars everywhere, up our drive, parked all over the close, across neighbours' driveways. Anna follows me around the side of the house, to the gate in the wall of fir trees. Everywhere is wet and dripping with cold. Fir fronds trickle water down the neck of my shirt. Anna follows, pushing the branches away reluctantly. On the other side is a path, slimy with mud. It feels good to have the cold searing my nostrils, reminding me I'm alive.

We walk away from the estate, out onto one of the rough fields, following the path we always take, up to the top. I try to start conversations about the cinema, some of the boys from school, but Anna is hard work. Someone is walking their dog in the distance; it bounds away and circles back again and again.

Even though it is creeping toward dusk and the sky is flinty, I can still see over to Blackmoss and the moors. From here, it looks like the torso of some sleeping giant.

I think about that empty, stale house, sitting up there. I remember the curve of the lane. The shout of the farmer and the sound of his fist. I remember the boy.

'When will you be moving?' Anna asks, reading my thoughts.

'Soon.'

'What's it like?'

'I've not been inside yet, but I don't like it. It looks tiny and it's miles away.'

There is a pause as we both stare out across the valley.

'It'll be OK,' she says.

But I know it won't. Now she's dead.

And then it comes, choking and sputtering up

through me. I puke over my wet shoes, the heat of my stomach steaming and soaking into the drenched grass. Anna holds my hair out of my face and rubs my back as I kneel down and retch.

CHAPTER THREE

A photograph inside the school reception shows an aerial view of the moors. It is a blue-black patchwork of peat and ochre grasses. You can trace the grey snake of a road as it makes its way from one city to another. There are hollow, silent places up there on the moors, and so many dramas: the walkers lost for good; the old World War Two planes, their metal skeletons still visible in between the dips and gullies of bogland; the lost souls of the dead; my mother's ashes.

I don't know why that photograph is in my head as Dad drives me to school. My first day back.

I never feel quite sure at school. I am the quiet one, the sensible one. I don't date boys. I do my homework. I keep my head down.

But everything has changed. After the worst thing has happened, what else is there to be scared of?

Dad drops me off. We are late and I hurry to my first lesson, English. As I cross the tarmac, I feel anxiety, like a ghost, spreading along my limbs, making me heavy and weak. I remind myself there's no place now for fear, for any feeling at all.

It is strange to look into the classroom: a dirty goldfish bowl, glass green, dank; the students hunched and bored in rows; my friends, my teacher, so separate from me.

As I sit down at my desk, Anna gives me a big smile.

I can lose myself in this world of pretend, just a story. Someone is reading. I relax into the sleepy calm behind a rectangle of a flecked formica desk, just listening, being normal. As though Mum is at work and I am here in the usual place at the usual time, doodling in the margin, coiling a wisp of hair loose from my ponytail.

'So where are we?' The teacher clears his throat. 'Lennie has just killed Curley's wife…'

Suddenly, there it is in the story.

Oh my God, I am crying. I'm in school crying. About a book. Because Lennie is dead, because George shot Lennie and he's dead. Anna is a wall to hide behind. If any of the others see me … crying in school like a bloody baby.

'Kay.' Anna nudges the arm I have curled around my face.

'No.' I am fierce.

Anna's brown eyes blink, completely out of her depth.

I can still be the same as everyone else, can't I? Just because my mum is dead, it doesn't mean I can't be part of the girl-ship: brushing hair, applying lippy, dawdling home, gossiping about school and boys... We are fifteen. Everything is new and exciting, isn't it?

Jess catches my arm as I walk through the gates with Anna.

'Party at mine on Friday!' She grins at us. 'Can you come?' She says this more to Anna than me. If Anna goes, I'll go. That's how it is. 'Mum and Dad are having a spa break. I've got to look after the dogs, soooo…?' She grins again, her eyebrows raised, and chews her gum deliberately.

Me and Anna look at each other, but it's me who looks back at Jess and says, 'What time?' We're in.

I'd never kissed a boy before Mum died. No, that's a lie; I once kissed Aamon McGinty from up the road. We were kids. We made a den in my bedroom and then lay under the blanket, and the sun through the woollen weave made a net of lines across our faces and our arms. He said, 'Close your eyes.' So I did. He kissed me. Once. On the lips. He said, 'Don't tell anybody.' So I didn't.

The party at Number 45, Ash Lane isn't really a party because there aren't enough people. It is a detached house in a cul-de-sac. The lights are on and music is pounding from the front room. I notice photos in the hall of Jess and her family: her, her brother and her mum and dad; manic grins, somewhere tropical. I wonder, what would it be like to have a brother? Someone to share all this with.

'Hi, babe, glad you came.' Jess envelopes me in a busty, perfumed hug, whispering, 'Might do you good,' into my ear. 'Did you bring any drink, babe?' she asks, more to Anna than me. Anna holds up a Spar carrier bag and the bottles of vodka and coke clink together. Jess grins. 'Told you the fake ID would work. There are glasses 'n stuff in the kitchen.' She points to a door.

I follow Anna. There are boys in the kitchen I've never seen before. They are playing, putting things in the microwave and watching the sparks. They turn toward us, and take in Anna's tight black dress, her smooth legs and heels. I'm used to Anna getting looked at; it happens often.

But what's new is that when I walk in, those boys

notice me. They see me too. The WKD bottles Anna and I sucked before we arrived have warmed my blood. So when one boy smiles over at me, instead of blushing and looking away, I hold his gaze and I smile back.

'Here.' Anna hands me a half-pint glass full of vodka and coke and grins.

'What?!'

I knock some back. It is warm but I don't care; then comes the burn at the back of my throat.

'How much vodka you put in here?' I gasp, laughing.

'Enough. Come on.' Anna tugs my sleeve and we go into the lounge. There are a couple of other girls we know; we all sit on the soft leather sofas and drink. The music is booming near my ear, so I don't really join in the conversation, I just enjoy the feeling in my stomach. It's the first time I have felt warm in days. I look down at my legs poking out from the short dress. We got ready at Anna's before we came out, and I am wearing one of her trademark tight numbers. The vodka makes me feel like I can do this, but my glass is empty.

'Anyone want another?' I ask. Anna gives me her glass without stopping talking and I head back to the kitchen.

Jess is sitting at the kitchen table with her tongue

down some lad's throat. The others are laughing as they line up shots. I don't feel drunk, but I do feel different. I take the vodka, what's left of it, and fill our cups with generous measures. It looks like all the coke has gone.

'Hey.' The lad grins at me, and holds up a lemonade bottle.

'Hey.' I nod and smile.

He pours some into the vodka. He has a cute smile. 'You from Jess's school?'

I can angle my head like Jess, and I can laugh – not too much, showing enough teeth, like I am in charge. I have something over this boy who has noticed me. I can rest my hand on my hip. I am smooth and drunk and perfect.

In the yard in the dark, I am alive when that boy puts his hands up my top. I am alive when he pulls my breasts out of my bra and sensation shoots through me.

A small pebble rocks in the alcoholic wash of my mind, a grain of resistance – perhaps this is not what I want, not how I want it to be.

What do I want? I want to fit in, to not be left out; I want to be accepted. Something inside me curdles and thrashes and attempts to right itself, like a beetle on its back.

And what does this boy do? I am falling towards him, for the soft feelings, the touch, the soporific heat of his hands on my skin. He pushes the cup of his fingers down the front of my trousers and my pants. He forces his fingers in and a sharp pain rips through me. I gasp. When I start to retreat, pushing him away becomes a game and he likes that and his tongue goes deeper into my mouth. The boy lies on top of me on the grass in the dark.

Jess opens the patio doors and sees us. I hear her retreating inside. 'You won't believe it! Kayleigh's out there with…' They fade to murmurs and laughing as the door slams and I know I have passed some test.

I stay at Anna's and go home in the morning. Mum's things are gone. Her shoes from the porch, the coats on the hook by the front door, even the one with her keys in; her handbag off the table. I don't know who has done it, Dad or Theresa.

I go straight into the bathroom and lock the door. There are clean, dusted spaces where her things used to be. Perfume, gone. Shaver, gone. I look in the mirror. I have an impulse to bang my fist against the glass, to see the bright colour of blood bloom, to turn my reflection into a mash of shards and silver.

I turn on the shower and pull my clothes off. They

stink of alcohol and I can smell him on me. I ache. For a long time I simply stand there in the water, a million threads of warm rain. Then I sit cross-legged under the force of the shower and close my eyes.

'Kay, are you going to be much longer?' Dad bangs on the door.

'What?'

'I need to use the bathroom.'

'Won't be long.' I sit there, keen not to leave my warm, wet shroud. But he bangs again.

'Kayleigh, please.'

I haul myself up, grab a towel and wrap myself up. Dad is waiting, arms crossed.

'Thank you,' he clips as he shuts the door, which says everything but thanks.

'Where have you put Mum's things?' I ask through the door.

He does not reply.

I peep inside their big wardrobe, a side for him and a side for her. Hers is empty. Someone has been here, extracted the parts of her, packed them up and shifted them off to junk yards, charity shops, jumble sales. Gone gone gone.

I change into clean clothes and lie on my bed. The sore space between my legs stings. Dad knocks quietly on my door.

'What?'

He pushes the door open and hovers in the entrance. 'We had to, Kay. We're moving.'

'Where?' I glare at him, daring him to say it.

'You know where, Blackmoss Lane. I get the keys next Monday.' His gaze slides away from mine.

I roll away, turning my back on Dad, until he gets the message and leaves me alone. I remember that day when they showed me the house at Blackmoss, on that tiny lane wriggling up the mountain. I remember the Land Rover and that man. I remember the lad with the dark eyes.

CHAPTER FOUR

We have to move house because we can't afford where we live anymore. The van comes at the weekend and three men tramp through our home, moving furniture first, then the boxes and bits. Dad barks at me, 'Hurry up.'

My period is late but there is no one to tell and nowhere in my head to process it. I leave the thought behind in our old house. We are moving on.

We drive in convoy, with the van behind us, the three miles to Furneston.

I never ask Dad about the farmer and whether anything was done, because I know it wasn't. No social worker went round to check on the lad, no action was taken over the damage to our car – Dad would have said. Mum deteriorated so quickly, everything else slipped through his mind. As we park the car outside 4, Blackmoss Lane, I can hear the distant barking of farm dogs.

Theresa is waiting for us. She gets out of her little red Corsa, brushing her hands down her immaculate jeans, and leans in to give me a wordless, brittle hug. I follow them up through the iron gate, up the cobbles to the two grassy stone steps. It is the first time I have been inside and I hate it already.

The house has dark rooms that smell of old people. It is a tall, squeezed sort of house, with a steep, dark stairwell thrusting up through its core. I wander into each room. I end up in the kitchen where Theresa has already set to work, disinfecting the inside of the kitchen cupboards. 'If we put the pans in this one,' she says, 'it'll be easier for you, you know, as they'll be nearer the stove.'

She is slopping water about. 'It won't be too difficult to organise. You can buy those ready meals some of the time, though they do tend to have a lot of fat in them.' I look at her stick-thin legs as she bends over to reach a spider's web in the cupboard. 'And at least you've got a dishwasher.' She smiles at me as though I should be really pleased. I hate her *youyouyou*, talking as though I'm the housewife, as though I am going to jump right into Mum's place.

I leave her to it and climb the steep stairs to my room.

It has the same smell as the rest of the house, and

faded floral spirals cover the walls. At least there's a decent view. I can see across the valley and see Blackmoss Lane disappearing up toward the mountain. The men start to bring boxes in marked with a 'K'.

I text Anna but there is no reply. I scroll through my social media accounts. Everyone seems to be out having fun, posting images of perfect lives. I can hear Dad downstairs watching TV. I feel this heaviness settling on my chest, making me breathless. It seems to fill my skin, like a darkness inside, pressing and pressing. I need to cry, but I can't; my eyes are dry with frustration and rage. I ball my hands into fists, pressing my nails into my palms tight, tighter. The pain concentrates into semi-circular marks as I lie there, wishing everything was different. Wishing I'd died too.

It's Maths first. I sit with Jess. 'Kay, look,' Jess whispers. She shows me a picture of a lad on her phone. He is only wearing boxers and shades. He looks hot, but full of himself, posing for the camera.

'My new man,' she grins. 'Lee. He's from town.'

'Nice,' I say. She flashes me a grin, a big Jess cheese, where her eyes get lost and she is all teeth.

'Marco keeps asking about you, y'know.'

'Yeah?' I feel sick hearing his name, but there is

no way I am letting her know that. This is the new me.

'Not interested then?' She taps her pen on the desk.

'Not right now.' I look out the window.

'Kayleigh Kay's got other fish to fry, methinks!' Jess crows. 'You're a right dark horse, aren't you?!'

I just smile, my face aching from the lie.

The next day I come on, fresh blood taking me by surprise when I'm at school. I have to borrow something from Anna to sort myself out. But I am so relieved. Lesson learned, well and truly. It won't happen again, I think, looking at myself in the mirror, putting my lippy on.

A few weeks later Anna and I are at the club. We've been drinking the JD and coke and I am turning and turning on the dance floor. Danny Hutton comes over to me and says he's fancied me since Year 7. I haven't fancied him, but he looks so pleased to be with me and I think, if I just could feel some warmth again…

We are kissing, sharing our saliva, our spit. But the world is turning and turning, the sick-sticky taste of whisky and coke round my mouth like a lipstick. Danny goes. There is no focus button for my eyes. The next one curls into my arms like sleep. He wants me to go outside, he is pulling and pushing, but I am dancing, turning under the gold and the black, and he leaves. The last flavour of the evening offers to walk me home.

He takes me the slow long way home, with dark places and low walls, and we are always stopping, his face is pushing into mine. I can't walk unless he steadies me. The alcohol is joy-riding round in my blood cells and the sky is dark and cold and there are no stars up by the swings as he pushes his hand under my dress.

I beeline to the house I live in. Not home. Never. Dad is asleep upstairs. We crawl into the living room in silence. There are photos of a dead woman called my mother and the dead rug and dead ornaments that she chose.

The only heat is that of the stranger.

Me and my friends meet up in the canteen in the morning but now I know things they don't know. I am flying above, looking down on the world. They talk about sex and boyfriends and getting pissed. It is only when Jess mentions the morning-after pill that I tune in. I have done it again. I can't even remember if we used anything. Heat blooms on my neck, creeping up onto my cheeks.

Careless, useless, stupid cow.

Anna notices my blush, misinterprets it and says, 'Gaz is talking about you.'

I look up. The boy from last night is outside, I can see him, unsure whether to come in. Good. I don't want him near me.

I say nothing. Anna can't mind-read at least. My friends raise their eyebrows and smile, like what I did last night is a joke, under my Dad's roof, as he slept, with that zit-faced boy outside, who wonders whether I'm interested.

'Poor Gaz,' Anna says to me, when the others have moved to get biscuits.

'Why poor Gaz?'

'He's really sweet. Don't you like him?'

I flush harder. 'What about you? You seeing Joe again?' I say, changing the subject. She leans forward, wrapping her fingers around the serrated cardboard cup, her cute little face split into a blossom of a grin.

'Hope so. He took my number. Nothing happened. You know, we only kissed.' She waits for a response. 'He's dead nice…'

'Nothing happened with Gaz either. He just walked me home.'

Anna sips again. Her drink is too hot. Tendrils of steam curl up and she blows them gently away.

Nothing happened.

CHAPTER FIVE

I skip school the next day. Dad doesn't know; he's already gone to work when I get up. I can't face it: Gaz. Anna going on. I try to go back to sleep but I can't, I am too restless. I forgot to put my stupid phone on the charger and it is completely dead so I can't even distract myself with mindless scrolling. I dig out the morning-after pill I bought yesterday. It was so expensive. I start to read the label; the sooner I take it the better. Low-level anger itches under my skin. I get up and swallow it down with water from the bathroom.

The house is so quiet, so still. In our old house you could always hear something – a radio, the sound of the neighbours going up the stairs.

The bedroom is smaller than my old one. It has a big window that overlooks the lane. My wallpaper is a kind of muted jade green, like leaves on the turn. If

Mum were here, we would make the house nice; redecorating, tidying, sorting. That thought weighs me down like a lump of tar.

I have to get out.

The March air is fresh and cool. The sharp smell of grass lifts and curls on the breeze. I pull the front door to with a satisfying slam and squint in the deluge of light. I can go right into the village or left up to the mountain. I look up.

The distant, endless bark of the dogs goes on and on. I haven't been up there since Dad's car got hit. The memory of that man is a sickly restlessness in the pit of my stomach. But now she is dead and I am scared of nothing. I feel a rush of adrenaline as my legs turn up the lane.

Behind Blackmoss, the true moors start, high and flat like a great shelf of heather and peat. Mum's ashes are scattered up here somewhere, off Hagger Tor, like she asked. I'm not even sure where we stopped that icy day, to watch the dust of her drift and float in the air, fall to the earth.

My legs enjoy the stretch and pull as I follow the road up to the mountain away from the house. The lane curves gracefully up, with sheep scattered in fields on either side, their mouths busy working the ground. The sharp grey cracks in the drystone walls look like they ought to contain messages or someone's hidden treasure. And that is all there is: no other houses or signs of life. No sign of the lad.

All the time I am saying to myself, I've got a right to walk here, that man can't touch me. Over and over. As I walk higher, looping up and round, I begin to see Beesley, my old town, in the distance. It is about two miles from Beesley to Furneston. The only difference, Dad says, is the train station. The rail link makes Beesley a more expensive place to live – but that doesn't matter to us because we have a car, he says. HE has a car. It makes all the difference in the world. Anna lives in Beesley, my only decent friend in the world. I am stuck up here knowing no one.

The lane ends with the forked track; one rutted, gravelled track dips down to the large farm a few hundred metres away, the second dirt track ends at a five-barred gate that marks the start of Blackmoss.

Rusty and a little bent, the gate has an impressive thick chain that clanks as I shift it. A padlock holds it fast, stopping anyone getting through. Dad said this was a public footpath, I'm certain. And anyway, so what? That man can't shoot me, can he?

I climb the gate and jump over, my heart awake in my chest. The grassy track on this side doesn't look as though any vehicle has been this way in years.

The wind makes me hunch my shoulders and pull my hands inside my sleeves. How big the space is up here. The sky feels wider. The base of Blackmoss slopes out of sight a mile or so in the distance.

Far from the gate, after I walk right along the rutted track curved round the side of the mountain, I see them.

At first they are silhouettes. One. Two. More. Their manes tangled and rough against the sky. Ponies, I suppose, from their height and size. Russet like the bracken; dust-coloured like the boulders strewn among the grass and heather. They are all still, watching me. Soft brown eyes, hooves paused, ears flickering, pert and attentive. I count six, then seven. One snorts and moves higher up, further from the path, turns her nose grass-wards and begins to bite at what scraps she can salvage.

'Hey,' I say softly to the one nearest me. Her off-white coat is thick with winter fluffiness, but beginning to shed. She eyes me skittishly. I can see the velvety hairs at the edge of her nostrils bowing with each quick, short breath. Her wide lips quiver. I so want to touch the slip of her coat and the rough of her mane, but when I put my hand out to stroke her, she neighs and scuttles her feet.

Anna started riding when we first moved to

secondary school. I joined her for a few lessons and it was fun. I learned to trot and canter, tack up, feed and groom. But then one day, there were no other ponies, so they made me ride Harvey. He was a giant palomino beast, nearly 16 hands. He looked down his nose at me, unblinking, his legs like tree trunks, his flanks great plates of muscle. Harvey lumbered along on the basic hack without giving me any trouble, until right near the end. Something spooked him. I think there was a rabbit or something in the long grass by the track. He started frisking back and rearing up. I couldn't tell you how I didn't fall off. The instructor calmed him down and I was fine. Never again though, I told Anna. I'd watch with respect and awe from the other side of the fence.

These ponies are different – small and sturdy. They have dipped their heads to forage. I long to touch one. I look about for any juicy grass to tempt them with, but all I can see is the hard, spiky mat-grass. I make a mental note to save some scraps for them from home, apples cores and stuff. I pat my pockets. I have half a packet of polos left. I wonder if they are anything like sugar lumps. It's worth a try.

'Hello,' I call gently. 'Here, horsey horsey,' I sing, feeling foolish.

They look sideways at me and flick their ears in

unison. I take a step forwards. The grey one snorts hard and backs away. The white one snorts too but doesn't move.

'Hey, what's this?' I hold my hand out with a couple of polos in my palm. 'Do you want it, eh? Sweetheart?'

I am a couple of steps away from her when she retreats, her feet twitching. The muscles in her flanks ripple, as though she is ready to flee.

'Hey, it's OK, *shush, shushhh,* now. It's OK. Look, I'll stay here.'

I stop, watching her. She shifts her body slightly so I am side on to her and she stills herself. She is blowing hard through her nose. I bow my head and gaze at her feet.

'Look. What's this? Do you want it. Here you are.'

She bends her neck so her head is closer to my hand. I don't move at all. I keep talking quiet nonsense as she sniffs. Then her front hoof steps forward half a beat and she can reach me. I can feel the bristle of her whiskers on my skin. It tickles. I grin.

'Like it?' I ask her, as she skips away, crunching the hard mints between her teeth. 'Good girl. Lovely girl.'

I take another step toward her, holding out another

mint. As I hand her the mint with my right hand, I gently place my left on her neck. She feels warm, and I realise how cold my fingers are.

Her lips grab hold of the mint in my palm and roll them towards her teeth.

'Oh, you are beautiful, aren't you?' I gently stroke my fingers along her neck, small unobtrusive movements, but enough to enjoy the feel of her coat and her wild smell.

She is almost white but covered in patches of dried mud. Bits of stick and heather are glued to her winter fur, which is coming out in places. Her mane is long and knotted, with yellowy streaks that fall into her liquid eyes. She looks at me and I drop my gaze.

'Here,' I say, and hand her the few remaining mints.

She is close up to me now and my shoulder brushes her shoulder, when suddenly her ears flick and her head rises, alert. She neighs and moves back a few paces. The herd gather and I wonder if I ought to have shared the mints.

'Hey!'

The shape of a person rises up from behind a boulder. He has a rifle in his hand. I see his car-crash of a haircut, the mud on his jeans, the power of his jaw, the fullness of his lips. I look into those same dark eyes.

'This is private,' he shouts out.

The ponies scatter out of sight. Small birds fling themselves out of the grass like stones hurled chaotically into the air.

'You've scared them, see?' He gesticulates in the direction of what, I don't know. The horses? The birds?

'You're not supposed to be here.' He hesitates, his voice quietening. 'It's private. Go on, go away.'

He pauses. I can see his T-shirt, a worn blue, moving with his pulsing breathing.

'This is private land, this is. This is my dad's land. Go on.' His voice has lost its momentum.

I do not move. He can't be that much older than me. I look at his beautiful face, frowning and wild. There is something else there, not anger but fear in his dark eyes. I wonder what strange world I've crossed into.

'Siôn! Where the hell are you?' Another voice. A voice I remember. Fiercer, rougher and coming closer.

'Go. Go on. It's my dad. You better go.' He stares behind him, then back at me. He looks panicked and afraid. 'Please.'

I go. Running, tripping over pockets of rabbit

holes and posies of weeds, sly stones rising up from the uneven ground. I stumble once, twice. I imagine them coming after me, the lad commanded by his father, but I daren't turn round. I vault the gate and am already down the lane, my breath ballooning, my throat grated sore from panting. I have to stop. I glance behind me. No one.

The sheep in the fields on either side of the lane raise their heads for a moment. Birdsong. Quiet, still air. Spring is coming and my heart is wild in my chest.

CHAPTER SIX

School is a nightmare. It is countdown to exams so that is all the teachers talk about. I can't keep all the stuff I am supposed to remember in my head, and I cannot see the point. What the hell do fractions or quadratic equations have to do with real life anyway? Dad says maybe I should take a year out; I can redo my exams next year. But that is even more depressing, like *Groundhog Day*, having to do it all over again but without Anna. Not that she's the same anymore. She has gone and fallen in love and every break-time I have to share her with Joe. It is so sick-making. Doesn't she know I need her?

'Want to meet up over the weekend?' I ask her, as we pack our things away at the end of another dismal Friday. 'I thought, watch a film or something? Cheesy chips?'

We always pig out on cheesy chips from the

chippy at the end of Anna's road. Her house is massive and always full of life. She has three brothers, two dogs and two cats. There is always different music blaring out, her dad's classical versus her eldest brother's tunes. There is always stuff on the stairs to trip over, or a dog lying stubbornly the length of the bottom stair. Everything looks a bit messy and her mum always looks a bit harassed. But she always greets me with a beaming smile. And there is always homemade bread to munch. I love it there.

'Oh sorry, Kay.' Anna pauses as she wrestles a mountain of books into her denim bag. She looks at me with pity. I hate that look.

'It's OK, just a thought. I should work anyway.' I grin at her, fake, to cover up my misery.

'It's just Joe's asked me…'

'It's fine.' I look out the window. 'Where you going this time?'

'Cinema. Don't know what we're seeing yet, we'll pick when we get there.' Her eyes are full of happiness. I am struck by how different our lives are now. A few months ago we felt like sisters. I still haven't told her about the boy on the mountain, Siôn.

'Look, let's go out Saturday, we'll do something. Why don't you stay over? A man isn't going to change my life!' She beams at me.

I feel mollified.

We don't walk together anymore now I am in Furneston. I have to either get a bus or walk. I don't want to get home any time soon so I decide to walk the two miles over the top. The view is fantastic from the brow of the hill; you can see into the valley I've left behind, and into the valley I have moved to. I wonder which school the boy from the mountain goes to. He looks about my age, but maybe he left last year. I'd have remembered if he went to our school. I wouldn't forget that face. There aren't any other secondary schools locally. There is only ours, unless he goes to the Catholic school, or the private one; or there's always Rutherton.

Rutherton is the school for those who can't behave, or won't behave. Dad is always being called there for some assault or other. He says it is really badly run, that the kids there don't stand a chance.

I have to walk into the tiny village of Furneston – it doesn't even have a shop – then out the other side, up the dead-end lane.

Our house is the second in a row of five houses, that look out of place on the edge of nowhere. Our house has not been cared for. Dad said the old couple who used to lived there have gone into a home. The front garden is better than the back, at least you can see where someone once took the time to lay out a flower bed and plant a couple of bushes.

I am hot after walking home and Dad still isn't in, so I change out of my uniform into jeans and an old T-shirt, make myself a glass of orange and sit out in the garden. I pick at some weedy patches in what used to be a path snaking through the grass. I can hear the neighbours talking through an open upstairs window. I feel in the way and try not to listen.

A Land Rover is tearing up the lane too fast. I recognise the engine, loud and rasping. This time a horse-trailer's attached. I want to rush inside, hide from them, but it is too late. All I manage is a low crouch against the doorpost. The farmer is frowning, his gaze fixed in front, his fat fists gripping the steering wheel. The lad from Blackmoss, Siôn, is in the passenger seat, his face close to the window. He looks at me, and … and then they are gone, with the smell of diesel spewing out up the lane.

A black cat leaps up onto next door's wall. I make a soft chucking sound and he comes over. His tail sticks up as he pushes his back against me and purrs loudly as I stroke him.

'Hello.' I smile. He winds himself in a figure of eight about my legs. 'Lovely boy,' I say, enjoying the feel of his warm soft little body against my skin.

'We used to have two, but one got run over.'

I look up to see an old man in a woolly sleeveless tanktop at the doorstep of Number 1.

'You the copper's daughter?' he says affably, nodding his head in the direction of our house.

'Yeah.' I smile and brush the dirt off my fingers. People always make a reference to Dad's job, like it gives him respect. Though what he does probably isn't what they imagine at all.

''E goes too fast.' He nods up the lane, where the Land Rover has left its diesel trail.

I look up toward the farm, but they're already out of sight.

'Croaker. The farmer up there. He's a shit. Sorry, love, but he don't take responsibility for 'owt.'

'No?' I rub between the cat's ears and he purrs vigorously. There is a pause. I shift my weight and the man clears his throat.

'He wants his dinner.' The man grins at the cat. 'You locked out?'

I shake my head.

'Bit quiet here for you, I 'spect.'

'Mmm.'

'There's no other young ones up here.' He gestures to the other cottages. 'Only Croaker's lad. But you won't want to hang around with 'im.' He laughs at the thought.

'No.' I say in an offhand way, though I am interested now. 'Is he trouble?'

'Not as such.' He pauses. 'He's a bit backward, I think. He wasn't in school at all for a while and you'd see 'im out in all weathers. I think social services went in.'

I look up the lane toward the farm. 'What about his mum?'

The old man crosses his arms. 'Croaker's wife ran off months ago, left the lad behind.'

'She left her son?' I stand up and cross my arms.

The man shakes his head. 'The lad's sixteen now so left school an'all. 'Ardly see 'im now, to be honest.'

I wonder about how he copes, up there with his dad. I wonder if he is lonely too. I feel a flicker of, what? Excitement? I want to see him again.

A woman appears on the doorstep behind the old man with her hands on her hips. She smiles at me and waddles down. 'Diane.' She gives me her hand to shake over the wall. She has fat fingers and blue eye shadow and looks me over without any embarrassment.

'I'm Kay.'

'You talking about Croaker?'

The old man nods.

'We're hoping they'll sell up soon, aren't we, Robert? An' bugger off someplace else. But most off, they don't bother us.'

He nods in agreement.

'Are the ponies theirs?' I ask.

'Think so.' She looks pointedly at her husband.

'They're lovely.' I remember the soft muzzle of the white pony, how she trusted me. I want to see them again.

'You feeding that cat or what?' Diane directs this at her husband. He rolls his eyes at me then chucks at the cat once more to make him come. The cat trots past him into the house.

'Nice to meet you, love.' She smiles again, then leans in toward me conspiratorially. 'Sorry about your mum.' She pats my arm. 'If you ever need 'owt, you know where we are.' She looks satisfied that she has brought up the matter and that is enough.

'Thanks.' It feels easier taking the pity from someone who never knew Mum, who doesn't know me.

They head inside, but I don't want to. I can't go into our house without feeling like I'm suffocating. I want to go back up the mountain. I remember the shout of the man, of Croaker, and the way I felt, running for safety.

I find Jess's number in my contacts. Jess's crowd aren't really me. I would never have thought of meeting up with her before. But I want a drink. I can fit in when I've had a drink. So I text her: 'U out later? Kxx'

A moment later, my phone rings.

'Kay!' I hear Jess stuffing her gob with crisps. 'Who's been skipping class this week?' she says, through a mouthful.

'I wasn't in the mood.'

'Kay, Kay! You are one of us after all!' she drawls and I hear someone else speak in the background. 'We're going to town later. You want to come?' I can hear other voices. They'll be round at someone's house getting ready, chilling out.

'Yeah, OK. When are you going?'

I hear background voices again, laughter. Has she got me on speaker phone?

'Marco'll be out too,' she laughs. 'I reckon he'll be up for some more practice.'

More laughter. Marco was my first time, at her party. I haven't seen him since, but the thought of bumping into him again, and worst of all bumping into him sober, is too awful.

'I don't think so,' I manage. 'I'll give that a miss. See you Jess.' I try to keep my voice light, then I punch the red button to cut her off. Tears sting my eyes as I stomp up the stairs. 'Silly cow.' I feel so angry at Jess, at me for being so stupid. For phoning her in the first place. She has never been a good friend; she isn't like Anna, but Jess is popular. She is always out and having a laugh, never letting anything get to her. It is a laugh at me this time. Naïve Kay who lost her virginity to that tosser. Well funny.

I send Anna a text: *Miss You Twonk x x*. I lie on my bed but no reply comes.

I find what I want easily enough. Dad always has beer in the house, but I know he keeps whisky too, for late-night tippling, he calls it, to unwind. Just what I need. I find a bottle in the sideboard, exactly the same place Mum used to put it in our old house. It's too easy.

I put some tunes on, not too loud; I don't want next door noseying round. I get some cola and mix it with the whisky in a coffee mug. It tastes raw going down, loads stronger than when I have whisky and coke in town. I don't dilute it though, slug it like medicine. Medicine to obliterate the sickness inside me. Me.

There is still no text from Anna. I know what I am going to do: go up on the mountain. See if I can see that boy again. The whisky is making me bold. Dad still isn't home, but he will be in a right mood if he comes back now and sees me drinking his best whisky. Share and share alike, Dad, I think.

I fill the rest of the coke bottle with whisky and stick it in a rucksack I had from when we went to Wales with school. I grab a jumper and head out the door. It clicks shut and I realise I don't have my key. I don't care.

I walk quickly up the lane to the gate. The views are beautiful; the sun is low in the sky and the air is clear and cool. Daffodils grow in random clumps along the hedgerow and the smell is delicious. I take another slug from the bottle. I'm not scared of a stupid farmer. What the hell is he going to do to me anyway, prosecute me? Do I give one?

I vault over the gate, slipping a little on the far side. There is no sign of the horses. It is a calm evening, very little wind, and I don't feel cold at all. Or maybe it's the whisky giving me false warmth. It feels good either way, away from everything and everyone. I walk off the track this time, up through the hard tufts of grass and hidden rocks, between the hunched bracken and the fuzz of heather. There is a low drystone wall, uncared for and broken in places. I reach it, out of breath and slightly dizzy, and lean against the millstone-grit boulders, covered in blooms of orange and green lichen.

I take a swig. It feels less intense now, easy to sup. I sit and look out over the valley, the distant chimneys from the factory, the glisten of sunlight on the belt of road joining Furneston to the city in the distance. You can't see my old home, my school, my old haunts from here, in the next valley along. So this is it, my new life, the new me, separated from it all.

The sun is beginning to set, turning the world pink. My loneliness weighs down on me. I lie on the grass and stare up into the navy sky. I wish I could stay there forever, like a stone in the wall, part of nature as the world moves on below. I feel hot tears stinging.

I hear a snorting sound that makes me catch my breath and my whole body tenses, until I register the ponies, slightly lower down the mountain. Their ears twitch and their tails flick as they work their way along, looking for anything edible.

I'm glad to see them, some other life up here. I call them over, but this time they do not come. I lay the apples in the grass and hope they will find them. The lad isn't about either, or if he is, he doesn't show himself. I keep hold of the thought of him, of the mountain and the ponies, like a light against the shadows as I walk home.

CHAPTER SEVEN

I wake up back in my bed where I collapsed when I got back; my arm crushed under me. My mouth tastes furry and my stomach dips and heaves like a ship in a storm. I roll over and groan.

It is light. My phone says 10.15 already. There's a message from Anna:

Fancy shopping? 12ish?xxx

I text: *Great. C u at urs?*

OK. We can catch the 12.25 xxx

A reason to drag myself out of bed.

I hear Dad come in. 'Kay? I've got some bacon. D'you want a bacon butty?'

'No, thanks,' I call. *Stompcreak stompcreak* down again.

The weight begins to lift. Knowing I'm not alone, someone is there, even if it's only Dad, makes a difference.

I rub my tummy. It flobbers about. I wonder if Dad will give me some cash so I can see what I can find to wear when we are out. I've been a size 12 for ages, but everything is getting tight on me. It is all the crap we are eating. I should ask Dad to get some more salad stuff. I wonder whether the ponies can eat lettuce and stuff? Anna will know what they can have.

After my shower, I put on my jeans and a T-shirt. I dry my hair properly, which I haven't done for ages, and even put some make-up on. I look OK, plain, but OK. I want a new look, something different, something that will shock. Short skirts, tight tops. Massive heels. I wouldn't dare, would I? It would be so un-me.

'I'm going to town with Anna,' I say, as I step down to the kitchen.

'Yes?' He's putting the shopping away. I fish out some biscuits from a bag, stuffing a Viennese whirl into my mouth and palming two more. Mum would have complained; there is already a packet open in the cupboard, we should finish those first. Dad doesn't even notice. I help unpack the rest.

'We can go out for tea tonight, if you like?'

'I might stay at Anna's.' My stomach swoops: does he feel like I do when he is here alone? Crippled by ghosts? 'If you don't mind?'

He looks at me. 'You never normally ask my permission!'

'I'm not asking you. I just thought…' I turn away and search for my black jacket.

'Do you need any money?'

I grin at him. He slips me £30.

'Thanks, Dad.' I hug him and feel his rough cheek graze mine. He smells homely, reminds me of all of us together, close and safe and warm. Just that makes me feel I'm teetering on the edge again.

The bus to Anna's is quiet, a few grey rinses in pairs, nattering over their shopping bags. My head is fluffy and everything sounds tinny.

I wonder when Dad will notice his whisky has gone and if he will say anything. I don't care if he does, I tell myself. I hid the bottle in the field for emergencies.

It doesn't take long for the bus to get to Beesley. Anna's is a big detached house; white and square and solid. It makes me smile, walking up the path, hearing the dogs barking and the music blaring. I can hear Anna and her brother's voices, raised and shouting. Even that is lovely noise to me.

I bang on the front door.

No answer, apart from the dogs increased manic

barking. They bash the door with their paws. I wait and eventually it opens. It is Anna's dad. He says nothing, but smiles and pushes the dogs away with his foot, as they threaten to engulf me.

'Hey, dogs,' I say and try to pat their heads. Their licky tongues get in the way, so I give up.

'Hush NOW, Prince. BELLA!!! Shush!' Anna's dad rolls his eyes at me and calls, 'Anna! Kayleigh's here.'

'Oh, hi.' She is at the top of the stairs. 'Come up. Bloody Paul's been in the bathroom half the morning so I'm not ready yet,' she grumbles, letting me past and shutting her bedroom door. She is half way through braiding hair up on each side of her head. She sits on the edge of the bed and I take over.

'Doesn't matter, we can get the train at one, we'll still have all afternoon. Do you want me to start again with this one?' I hold up the first braid and look at her in the mirror. She nods. 'How was the film?'

'Good.' She grins at me.

'Did you see much of it then?' I smile.

'Some of it,' she says shyly. 'Oh, Kay, he is sooo lovely. Look.'

Anna holds up her wrist. It has a charm bracelet with a love-heart charm dangling down.

'Ooh, that's gorgeous.' I lean over her to see it.

'He must really like you.' I carry on collecting the strands of Anna's thick hair. The light shines through it and it looks almost red. She would hate me for saying that. It glows like a warm fire. I love the colour of her hair.

'He said it's an anniversary present.'

'Anniversary?!' I snort. 'Do you want them together at the back?' I curl the braids back away from her face.

She nods. 'We've been seeing each other for a fortnight now.'

'Oh my God, so what is he going to do – get you something every two weeks then?! He'll be skint!'

'No!' She is stung. Her eyes glance down and I feel mean.

'Ignore hopeless me. You're lucky.' I smile at her. 'Done.'

She looks at her hair and twirls. 'Thanks, Kay.' She hugs me and catches my cheeks, squeezing them between her palms. 'You'll meet someone soon; someone who deserves you.'

We walk up to the train station and wait on the platform. I tell Anna about Jess and what she said on the phone.

'You know what she's like.' Anna is checking her

messages and not looking at me. 'She can be a right bitch sometimes.'

'She is a bitch.' I fold my arms tightly.

'You two are always falling out though, Kay. You'll make up again soon.'

I don't answer. The station is busy now: kids from school, Saturday shoppers, mums with prams and grizzling kids. The train is coming into view when I see him: the boy from the mountain.

'Look, Anna, look!' I prod her.

'What, what am I looking at?' she says loudly.

'Shhh!' I roll my eyes. 'Honestly.'

What is he doing waiting for our train? He is dressed in loose jeans and a black T-shirt with a white plastic bag rolled up in one hand. His hair is damp and his fringe flops into his eyes. He jumps into the end carriage.

'Come on.' I drag Anna with me.

'What are you doing?'

'This carriage. Come on!'

She follows me, complaining, as we find two seats, sharing a table with an elderly lady. 'This one's much more crowded. What is it?'

'Him up there,' I whisper, nodding. 'Look, the one in the black top.'

'What? That scruffy one?' she whispers.

'What do you think?'

She looks again. He has his head down and is picking a hole in the plastic bag. 'It's hard to tell. I'll watch him when he gets off. Why? Who is he?'

'My neighbour.'

It isn't far into town. At the last stop, everyone is getting off. We have a good chance to look at him as he stands waiting at the next door down. He keeps his eyes on the floor. He is slim, but you can see the brown skin of his arms and the muscles in his forearms. He has real bedhead hair, but I think it looks kind of cool, in an unfussy sort of way. We follow the rest of the passengers off the carriage and down onto the platform, through the ticket barriers.

As he is about to walk outside, he turns and looks right at me. I feel my stomach swoop. It is only for a moment. He doesn't smile, but throws me a lost look and then lopes out of sight.

'Did you see, did you see?' I pester Anna.

'He's very good looking,' she says reluctantly, as we follow the crowd out into the sunlight.

'But?' I ask, scanning the shoppers to see if I can still spot him. I have the mad idea of following him, though I don't really know why.

She shrugs. 'Dunno. Looks like his hair needs a good brush.' She makes me laugh.

I haven't felt this good for a long time. We have loads of laughs and I feel like I've got Anna back again. Not that I want her all to myself, and I am glad she is happy with Joe, but I need her in my life.

I buy some new stuff, a short skirt and a tight top. 'Tarty, yet tasty,' Anna says.

'Let's go out tonight,' I plead, when we lie on her bed resting our aching shoppers' feet. 'Come on. Now we have ID we can get served anywhere.' I rest my chin on my palm.

'I haven't got any money; I'm all spent up.' She waves her hand at the shopping bags. 'Let's watch some crap on the telly. You can stay here tonight if you like.'

I glower out the window, not speaking.

'Look, it's nearly your birthday anyway. Let's save up and then we can go to the Kube again, have a blast on the JD and coke. It'll be loads better. Seriously, Kay, I'm skint now and I can't ask Mum for any more. I'm horse riding tomorrow.'

I don't have much money left either, but want to try out my new gear and have a dance.

'She's doing a roast tonight as well. Yummy scran?'

I glance at her.

'C'mon, I'll go and ask Mum if it's OK.' She shifts off the bed and goes out.

Her mum pops her head round the edge of the door. 'Hiya, Kay.' She smiles at me, warm and kind.

'Hi,' I reply, sitting up against the pillows.

'How are you settling into the new house?' She comes to sit on the edge of the bed. I shrug. 'It's tough you being out of the village now, isn't it?' She looks at me with her eyes all sympathetic, but not fake, real, like she means what she says. And that's all it takes. I can't reply or I will cry. There's this empty hollow inside of me, and I'm standing on the edge, about to fall in. I manage a 'mmm'.

'Well, you know you are welcome to stay here any time you want, you don't need to ask. You're always welcome.' She stands up and smooths down her skirt. 'See you in a bit. You like roast pork?'

'Yes, thanks,' I manage. She smiles again and is gone.

Anna's mum is nothing like mine. Anna's mum is really mumsy. She wears floral skirts and seems to spend all her time doing housey stuff. She doesn't have a job, except for looking after them all, I suppose. I like that she is so different. It makes it easier to see her. My mum, before she got sick, she was always out of the house. She worked at the hospital. Seems ironic really – she spent years caring for sick people and then she gets sick herself, and no medicine or nurse or doctor can make a bit of difference.

Anna sits next to me on the bed. 'It's OK to cry, you know, Kay. You must really miss her.'

I can't show her though. I hold my head down, flat against my arm and feel the damp patch spreading. She lies across me and strokes my hair, then goes to get a tissue.

'We can download a film, if you like. Shall I see what there is?'

She looks online and I take a deep breath and claw my way back from the edge. I feel like after I've been swimming. As though it would be impossible to lift myself off the bed for the meal, never mind go out somewhere. I text Dad to tell him where I'll be staying. He never replies to texts, but at least he will read it and know I am OK. When Anna's mum calls up, the smells make my stomach curl up at the sides with hunger.

It is delicious, and funny too. Callum and Danny, the younger boys, fall on the roast potatoes like they are starving.

'Share, boys,' Anna's mum says.

'Honestly, see what I have to put up with,' Anna says. 'Pigs.' She makes her eyes go all narrow.

'Hey, Mum, do you know what pig is in French?' Danny says with his mouth full.

'Porc,' quips his dad. He raises his forkful of dinner in Danny's direction.

'No, it's *cochon*.'

'Is it, dear? Well, you are learning lots of new things now, aren't you?'

'Mum, he's not three anymore.' Paul groans.

'You're all still my babies.' She winks at me.

They are arguing as usual, but not in a nasty way. I like their banter. Paul is all sarcastic and thinking he is all grown up, but his dad can still catch him out. I don't join in, but I laugh along and they make me feel part of it all.

'Mum, can we leave the table now? We've finished,' Anna asks, after we've stuffed ourselves on homemade apple crumble and custard.

'Sure.'

We slob out on Anna's bed and watch some comedy film. It isn't very good but it is quite funny in places. I think Anna has picked it to try and cheer me up. I feel better than I have since the funeral. I wonder how Dad is feeling. Saturday evenings, him and Mum usually went out for a meal, even to the theatre or cinema sometimes. They had friends but they are all couples and he never goes out with mates on his own. I don't even know if he has any.

'Thanks for tonight, Anna, I'm glad we didn't go out after all.' I curl up in the duvet, drifting close to sleep.

'We'll have a good night on your birthday, I promise,' she says. 'You're my best mate, Kayleigh Kay.'

'You're mine too, Anna Twonk.'

'Oy!'

I grin as she whacks me with her pillow.

She falls asleep first and I lie cosy and warm in a duvet cocoon, drifting off to the noises of her family talking and shifting about in the other rooms.

I open my eyes but I still can't see. It is black. I can feel the duvet against my arms and legs. I grope about wanting to call out, but I can't get enough air through my nostrils so I open my mouth wide and try to gulp it in. It's like the air isn't working; the darkness is filling my mouth. I cannot see my hand in front of my face. There is no light, not a sliver round the door, or through the curtains. My phone. I reach around for it by the bed; something falls to the floor. Fear snares my lungs and squeezes them tight.

'Mum, MUM!'

'Kay?' A voice murmurs next to me, and then a bedside light is on, flooding the room. Anna is blinking at me, her forearm shielding her eyes from the brightness.

'Bad dream?' she murmurs, patting my arm.

I let my breathing return to normal. She leaves the light on and falls immediately back to sleep. I lie awake until daylight blooms.

CHAPTER EIGHT

The next couple of weeks the pressure of exams is worse than ever. The teachers keep getting us to read and reread all our notes. I still don't have a clue what course to do next. I used to like Science, but none of my friends are doing it. I know that shouldn't make a difference, but it does.

My birthday looms ahead: April 4th. I'll be sixteen. I have never felt less like celebrating. The thought of Dad trying to buy presents is excruciating. All the little things Mum used to get for me, there will be none of that. And without her there... I don't want to think about it.

'Hey you, gonna be sixteen and legal soon,' Jess grins at me.

I glower at my Maths revision book.

We have been paired up for Maths and the thick teacher has stuck me with Jess. She sits there, big sovereign ring glinting on her finger.

'Aw come on, Kayls, you not still mad at me about that call, are you? It was only a joke. I thought you liked Marco. He really fancies you.' She pats my hand. 'Come on.'

'No, he's a tosser.' I move my hand from beneath hers. 'I can't stand him.'

'OK, OK.' She folds her arms. 'Look, I lost my cherry to someone I don't like too. It doesn't matter.' She looks out of the window. 'It's over and done then. It doesn't have to be such a big deal.'

She looks blank and far away, and I don't believe her. It did matter to her and it mattered to me. 'Who to?'

'No one you know,' she says. 'You know me, Kay, I don't mean offence. I'm just all gob. Lads are bastards. Don't let's fall out over them. We girls got to stick together.' She pats my hand again.

'Yeah, you and your gob.' But the corners of my mouth lift into a smile. 'Your cherry?!'

And then we are both cackling until Mrs Whitshall clears her throat with a, 'Revision, girls.'

Friday 4th April. My sixteenth birthday.

I was born at 1.40 in the morning. Mum told me.

I wake up and look down my bed. Nothing.

There was always a small pile of gifts waiting for

me to open. I told myself not to be disappointed. I knew Dad wouldn't do things the way Mum did. But knowing I shouldn't be disappointed doesn't mean I'm not. I slope down the stairs, wanting to pretend it is simply a normal day.

'Happy birthday, love.' Dad is already there. He makes me a brew and gives me a plastic bag. He hasn't wrapped it. When he asked me what I wanted I said jewellery. 'I hope you like it, Kay. You know I'm not the best shopper.'

'Thanks, Dad.'

I open the bag and inside there is a black velvet jewellery case. The lid pops open with a satisfying sound. Inside is a fat silver bracelet. It is patterned with some kind of Celtic design. I wouldn't have picked it: it is too big, too much, too clumpy looking. Trying to compose my face, I hug him. But his eyes search mine out. 'Do you really like it, Kay? We can change it if you don't?'

'I do. I love it.' I try it on, swivelling it over my fingers onto my wrist.

'Are you going to have some breakfast?' he asks, walking out of the room. I can hear him rustling in the kitchen.

'Yeah.' He hasn't bought me anything else. I didn't think I had any secret hopes, but I had. I'd hoped that

Dad would be… Be what? Like Mum? As if that could ever be.

'I'm going out tonight, Dad, with Anna.'

He returns holding a card.

'Thanks.' I open the yellow envelope. It says, '*To a Darling Daughter on her Birthday,*' with some flowers painted on it. Inside Dad has put £50 and written, '*To Kayleigh, all my love, Dad xxx.*'

I hug him, trying not to cry.

'Sorry it isn't very special, love. I didn't know what you want. Your Mum did all the birthday stuff…'

'I know, it's OK. I can buy some new clothes. Thanks.'

There is a card from Theresa with a cartoon of a girl with loads of shopping bags. '*To a special Niece.*' And a note saying she will give me her gift at the weekend.

'Where are you going?' Dad asks as he ties his tie in the hall mirror.

'Just out.'

'You're still not old enough for the pubs, Kay.' His reflection catches my eye.

I huff. 'Don't worry. I'll be fine. I'll be with Anna.' And bloody Joe as well, I bet. 'Bye, Dad.' I kiss him on the cheek and he hugs me tight.

'Do you want a lift today?' he asks as I slip away from him.

'No, it's OK, thanks. I'm meeting a mate on the bus,' I lie, not looking at him. I don't want to be so close to him all the time. I'm not used to it.

Does he look disappointed? There is something in his eyes that makes me feel I'm letting him down.

It's a fine spring morning, hardly any wind, as I walk to the bus stop in the middle of Furneston. I feel myself cheering up as home disappears. It is not about the past, it is about me and my mates. Here and now.

I want to look good, feel good. I want that drinking high. Maybe a few smokes. I am getting ready at Anna's and then we'll meet Jess and the others in town. I've got my going-out stuff I'll leave in my locker at school: the top, skirt, some heels Jess has lent me, make-up, and straighteners, as Anna's are broken. I'm sixteen and I am going to have some fun.

'Happy birthday!' Anna grins at me during registration. 'You can have your card now, but the present's too BIG to bring to school!'

'Ooh, thanks!' The card says, *Reasons I love my best mate Kay lots and lots*. Inside there is a list: one of the points, with a picture of two stick people with wine glasses, says *'cheeky wines'*.

'Tonight!' I grin.

She has written inside it: *'You are my bestest mate*

in the whole wide world and I'm always here for you,
love you loads Anna Twonk xxxxxxx.'

A few others come over and hand me cards and make a fuss of me. It really cheers me up.

School drags all day but finally the bell goes and you can hear the scraping of chairs in classrooms, the swinging open of doors, and see the stream of red and black uniforms outside the window.

I have McDowell for Science last lesson and he treats us like twelve year olds. We are all having to wait behind our stools till he's counted the equipment. Some loser has decided to try and rob a Bunsen burner so we are still waiting. 'Who wants a Bunsen burner anyway?' I roll my eyes at my neighbour.

Eventually one of the lads gives the Bunsen burner back, and McDowell lets us go after a lecture about safety. Again.

'You've been ages.' Anna is leaning on the railings at the bottom of the drive with Joe.

Joe whispers something in her ear and she smiles. 'See you laters,' he says, kissing Anna on the mouth.

'Bye!' She grins as he walks backwards away from her, turns and is gone. I have her attention.

'God, Science! McDowell being a control freak, as usual.'

We trail up the hill to Anna's house. It isn't far

from school and we are soon being assailed by the barking dogs.

'Shut up, dogs!' Anna shouts.

Anna's mum is baking in the kitchen. 'Hiya, love. Good day? Kay! Happy birthday.' She leans over her daughter to give me a hug.

'Thanks.' The scent and female softness. I blank.

'Sixteen now! So grown up. I hope you girls are going to be sensible tonight.'

'We will.' Anna pats her mum's cheeks. 'Two drinks and then home.' She winks at me. I try to refocus on where we are, what we are doing, what I should be feeling.

Anna's mum continues sifting. 'Make sure you do. I'll wait up, you know. Casserole for tea and no arguments. You need some food to soak up those two drinks. OK?'

I smile. Anna's mum is so relaxed.

'Anyone else meeting up with you?'

'Jess,' I say as Anna pours milk into steaming mugs of tea.

'And we'll probably bump into Joe at some point.' She pops down toast into the toaster and doesn't look at me.

Joe? It's *my* birthday and I don't want to see bloody Joe.

There is an awkward pause. Anna cries out, 'Present!!!!!!' She bounces up from the table and out of the room. She returns with a square gift wrapped in pretty gold paper with purple birds flying in and out of twining leaves. It even has ribbons and a gift tag. *'To Kay, love from Anna.'*

'I know it's not that big but I didn't want it to get all squashed at school.' She smiles expectantly. 'Go on then, open it!'

I don't want to tell her this is the first present I've had today which has been wrapped; that I want to savour the neatness of it. All those Christmases and birthdays past, with the gift-giving and the opening, seeing my pleasure reflected in Mum's face; the memories come like flashes, catching at my heart. It is true: you don't know what you've got until it's gone. I cannot think of it. I cannot.

The paper rips easily and I see underneath the Clinique logo. It is a box of make-up. 'Wow, a proper brush,' I say, holding up the foundation brush. 'Anna, these are really expensive.' I lift up pots and tubes and lipstick.

'It should be the right shade,' she says, as I turn the foundation bottle over in my hands. 'We can always swap it though, so long as it's not opened.'

'It looks perfect. Thank you sooo much.' I reach

over and hug her. Joe might be joining us later, but it doesn't mean Anna doesn't want to spend time with me. It will be a good night. I know it.

'Mum got some money off with a voucher or something, and we thought you need a pampering.'

'We can get done up properly now. You do me and I'll do you.' I smile.

Anna has a bottle of fizzy wine. Her mum has actually bought it for us. It is only 6% proof, but still. After an early tea and homemade birthday cake, we go upstairs to get ready.

The wine is cold and sweet and makes me feel good.

Anna is trying really hard not to talk about Joe, but eventually she moves on to her favourite subject as she is putting colour on my eyelids. I watch her in the mirror through one eye. As she is talking she takes up the mascara brush and begins on my lashes.

'He thinks he's ugly! It's funny because I always thought it is just us girls who do that, but it's not, is it?' She pauses, with the mascara brush in the air. 'Look, brown's better than black with your skin colour.' I nod. 'It's not just us that have insecurities at all.' She is pleased with herself at this revelation. 'You're done.'

I look properly in the mirror. I don't look like me. I look older and my eyes seem bigger. She's done a good job.

'My turn.' She jumps into the chair after me. 'You mustn't say anything, because he made me promise I wouldn't tell anyone.' She hesitates. 'Even you, he said. But I can tell you anything, I know, so…'

'Course. You know me, I don't gossip.'

She pauses. I start putting the foundation on with the brush, gentle sweeps across her cheeks. 'Well, he used to think his – his *dick* is too small.' She waits to gauge my reaction.

I laugh. 'All boys think that!'

'No, he is really worried about it. But I told him it's just fine. I don't want a lad with an enormous one anyway, it'll hurt.'

'Oooh,' I tease her, 'so you've seen it then!'

'We haven't done it yet. We've just touched each other. He's OK with us taking it slow. I want to, but I'm a bit scared.' She pulls a face.

'Well, remember to BE CAREFUL!' we both say in unison, then fall about laughing. It's what our Health Education teacher always says at the end of a sex ed. lesson.

Everything feels great. Me and Anna against the world. No Joe can spoil this.

'Oh, don't you two look beautiful,' Anna's mum gushes as we sashay down the stairs. 'Much older than you are, mind you.' But there's humour in her

70

eyes. 'Look after each other now, and no splitting up, OK? Not for anybody.' This is aimed at Anna.

'Mum!' But she allows her mum to kiss her. I am offered a hug too, and I am in such a good mood it doesn't make me sad. This is my night.

It is great at first. We meet up with Jess and her crew. There is no sign of Joe. Everyone is buying me drinks and making a real fuss of me. Marco and his lot turn up, and I don't care. He keeps looking at me, and I know it, but I am not going there. I have no trouble getting served, and at the bar a fella in a suit looks me up and down and makes this face like he's impressed. It's embarrassing, he's so much older than me, but it is flattering too. I feel on top of the world walking to our table. Sixteen. This is only the beginning.

We are in the Rose and Crown when the atmosphere begins to turn sour. It's about 10ish and we are on the cider and black. Jess and her crew have been in a great mood, but then something kicks off with one of the lads. He gets thrown out and so they all leave. All of a sudden the place seems empty. Me and Anna huddle round our drinks. 'Shall we go too?' Anna suggests.

'Where?'

'We could just go straight to Kube?'

I know why Anna is keen to move on, to see bloody Joe.

'I want to go to the Slug and Lettuce,' I grumble. The college lot go there. I am too shy to approach them. Jess always gets the conversations started. I have a vague idea in my head that the boy from the mountain might be there. Though I know he won't be.

'The Kube'll shut doors, won't it, if it gets too busy? And we want to bust some moves, don't we?!' Anna wiggles and slops some of her drink onto her top. 'Oh no,' she grins, all lopsided and endearing.

The Slug is the opposite direction and my feet are already killing in these shoes.

'Ohhhhkay,' I groan melodramatically. But I am irritated. I know the night isn't about me anymore.

As soon as we are through the door, Joe comes over. 'Happy birthday, Kay!' He hugs me in an arms-length sort of a way. I wonder if Joe is fanciable, as he and Anna are making their hellos. He isn't one of the lads from school we've lusted after, but he is kind of cool in an understated way. It is the way he walks. It is weird how I've never noticed before.

I look away as Joe and Anna twine themselves round each other. Jess is in here too, with some lad. I go to the bar to get a round in. I want to dance, but not on my own. I want to be in that place where I don't care. The sweat on the walls makes me feel a bit queasy.

'Here,' I say, bumping Anna's arm.

She reluctantly turns to me. 'Thanks, Kayls.' She takes a sip.

'Come on, have a birthday dance with me.'

'Next song, next song.' She plants a sticky kiss on my cheek. 'Why don't you dance with Leeso?'

Leeso, Joe's best mate, is on the dance floor on his own, going for it. I look at his shirt: too neat. He has a nervous energy that makes him look like he's trying too hard. I sit and watch and drain my whisky and coke.

Eventually she dances with me, but I have lost the mood by then. The music is tuneless and I can't get into it. I feel wooden and uncoordinated. The lights show up the smeared make-up on Anna's eyes, the dark patches under the armpits of the lad dancing in on me, dust and moisture threading in the air. I wish I could click my fingers and be cosied up on the camp bed in Anna's room.

'Pee stop,' Anna mouths and totters off up toward the loos. I ought to go with her, but don't want to hear all about how wonderful Joe is again. I know I will say something cruel. I sit down.

Joe is there. He's been watching us dancing. He doesn't smile at me. It is awkward. I've never spoken to him on his own before. I feel sour and pissed.

He leans across to talk over the music, but I don't expect what comes out of his mouth.

'You don't like me, do you,' he says into my ear. The music is loud and his breath is hot and close on the skin of my neck. 'You don't like me being with Anna. But you're gonna have to get used to me, you know.'

He pauses but keeps his mouth close to my ear. I feel sick.

'Soon she's gonna like me even more than you.' A pause again. My head feels muzzy. I can feel the heat radiating off him, the smell of the booze on his breath. 'I think you fancy her yourself. I've seen the way you look at her.' He moves back slightly to grin at me, smug, almost bitchy.

Retaliation fizzes up. I talk into his ear; spite and bitterness.

'She will never like you more than me,' I say, but my stomach is knotting with anxiety. I know how to wipe that ugly smile off his face. 'She tells me all your secrets.' Now it's me looking smug.

He looks away, trying not to show that I have got to him. I move in once more.

'Poor *little* Joe.'

And he knows what I mean.

'Fuck off.'

'That's what she says,' I crow. 'Poor little Joe.'

I have hit the spot. I lean over to try and get eye contact. He pushes me off with the side of his arm. Briefly my breast catches against his arm. It wasn't intentional but I can feel the heat where his arm brushed me.

'You're just a slut.' He relishes the word. 'That's what she thinks of you.'

He stands up now, eyes level, while I pretend the word doesn't sting. A perfect word for me, one I use myself.

Now I am the worst part of myself, a snarling, bitching witch, and I do what can only hurt me the most.

I take hold of his arms.

'And you'd love a bit of this slut, wouldn't you?' I move towards him. At first there is no resistance.

And then he shakes himself free and firmly pushes me away. He looks into my eyes, triumphant.

Anna has returned.

She doesn't speak to me or look at me. She snatches up her bag and walks. Joe is gone too. Out of the door and into the night.

I look round to see if anyone has seen. No one else cares. Jess has gone. Joe's mate has gone. There are simply nameless faces, sweaty, pissed, out of it.

I go to the toilet and sit in the cubicle, squeezing my nails into my palms, until someone starts hammering on the door.

'Hurry up, else I'm gonna piss on the floor.'

I slam open the cubicle door. The woman steps away, surprised, but I am gone before she says anything. I don't care.

It is his fault, stupid little git winding me up. What does he mean, *I bet you fancy her yourself?* Wanker.

I leave the Kube full of purpose. I walk away from the town centre, pleased to be leaving it all behind.

'I'll keep you company, love!' some fella yells from the taxi queue. I walk faster. As it gets quieter and the street lamps more infrequent, I urge myself to go on, into the darkness, raging, daring the fear to come. A man passes by on the other side of the street, his bulky coat making him seem enormous. I wrap my arms round my chest trying to cover up as much skin as possible. I walk faster.

It would serve me right if I was raped and murdered. Serve me right for being such a total bitch. I am jealous, that's all. Jealous because Anna has some love and affection in her life and my life is empty and crap. The only decent thing in it is Anna and now I've deliberately fucked that up.

The tangerine glow of the streetlights makes small acidy pools on the pavements. Every time I walk through one, the darkness seems denser than before. I get my phone out and use it like a torch, but all it does is make the dark thicker and light me up. I turn it off. Every now and then a car moves past, its sharp lights making shadow figures out of the hedges. My heels are beginning to blister my feet. The anger begins to relent and in its place a prickling shame clusters in my chest.

I reach the T-junction where the lane to Furneston goes through the wood. There aren't any street lamps to light the way, only the orange glow from the town. I stand at the edge of the dark. Fear beats the drum in my chest faster and louder. But rage flickers up again.

I walk into the blackness. Come on then, someone. Get it over with. I want this to end.

All that happens is I get tired; too exhausted to think. The alcohol wears off and leaves me trudging through the dark until I reach the main road. I drag my feet, aching, freezing.

I see something – a fox. It hurries across the road.

Its eyes glint silver at me before it melts into the verge.

Each step is a step closer to home, to safety and my bed.

I wonder if Anna got home OK. Joe will have made sure she did. What will her mum say at Anna leaving me? Will Anna tell her why?

I turn up Blackmoss Lane, but I can't make it any further. I land heavily on the verge, on the overgrown spring grass. I am wet from the dew and cold to the bone.

It has been ages, minutes, I can't tell. A shadow walks into the faint patch of light where the lane meets the main road. Someone else is coming up Blackmoss Lane in the middle of the night.

I shudder. I tuck myself into the low ditch.

The person is moving fast, steady and quiet, barely making a sound on the gravel. I am sober now; too aware of how I must look, hiding in the long grass at the edge of the road, like some wild animal.

It's him. It is the boy from the mountain. I can tell by the way he shakes his head slightly to get the hair out of his eyes.

I want to say something. Something simple: hello. He is oblivious to me and my voice is broken. I see him moving away, getting smaller, but then something,

I don't know what because I don't think I've made a sound, makes him stop in his tracks. He turns. His eyes run over the verges either side of the lane, then his gaze locks with mine.

CHAPTER NINE

'I thought you were a badger,' he says, as he stands over me.

I try to make myself look casual, as if that's possible at god-knows-what-o'clock in the morning, sitting in a ditch. 'Just having a rest.'

He holds his hand out to me, his warm brown fingers grip mine briefly, and I am up again. Rough palms, smooth knuckles I can feel in my fingertips.

'You're shivering,' he says, as we walk up the lane. He takes off his jacket and I put it on without complaining.

'Thanks,' I mutter.

'I saw you today on the train. You've moved into Number 2. Your dad's got a Volvo Estate. Crimson.'

I look up at him briefly. He has broad, rich lips. I can see the mercury pools of his dark eyes, black in the night. He doesn't seem to expect a reply, and I am glad. I nod and watch my feet, making sure they are going forward, not tripping, keeping straight ahead.

'You been in town too?' I ask eventually, wanting to hear him speak again.

'Town? No, I've been down in Barker's Wood. There's a badger set there and her babies are just starting to come out.'

'Badgers?'

He turns to me, a gentle smile edging onto his face. 'By next month they'll be even more lively.'

I am bemused. I spent my whole evening stuck in hot stinking bars, and he was out in this clean cold. I breathe in the earthy damp air, sharp against my nostrils. His jacket has a stronger smell, bark and leaves.

'It's my birthday today,' I say.

'Happy birthday.'

'It's been shit.'

He looks at me, a darker look now. The lost look from the train. 'How old are you?'

'Sixteen. You?'

'Eighteen in August.'

We walk in silence. I am barely able to see the lane. The whole world is just shades of dark. I follow his sounds, the step of his trainers, the brush of clothing; I follow the warmth of his body.

'I'm Kay,' I tell him, to break the silence.

'Siôn,' he returns. Then nothing. I feel awkward.

He stops. Listening. I automatically halt too.

'What have you heard?' I move a little closer. Then I hear it, the croaking of frogs.

'They lay their spawn in the ditches here. Last year it was too dry and most of the tadpoles died.' He carries on walking.

The three street lamps that light our odd row of cottages come into view, their glow helping to orientate me. It is like a small piece of civilisation marooned in the darkness.

I can see him better now, his profile, the straight nose, his lips. I want him to speak again.

'You like animals,' I say.

The light catches his cheekbone, reflecting in his eyes like a cat's. 'More than people, usually.'

We are at my gate. We stand. Awkward. Then I remember, the jacket.

'Thanks.' My shoulders are cold as I return it to him, the scent of him leaving me.

'Bye,' he says.

I walk to the door and he turns toward Hagg Farm, with the same swift, silent gait. I watch him, the glow of light on his hair, until he is gone.

I shut the door quietly behind me and turn my key to lock it once more, kick off my shoes and creep in, hoping Dad won't wake. But I can't hear his usual snoring from the bedroom. The house is cold and silent; he isn't home. Where is he? It's too much. I am too tired even to cry. I peel off my damp clothes and crawl into bed. I've never felt more lonely in my life.

I wake to a bright day with a jolt. I sigh and try to sit up in bed. My feet ache. My head aches. I lie down again, pulling the covers up over my head, making a cocoon. I am still wearing my clothes from last night. I need a shower. The covers need changing; they smell stale.

I close my eyes and try to sleep once more, drift into nothing. My body is heavy, but my mind… Why am I here and not at Anna's?

The darkness; walking without shoes; Anna's face. A memory of my hands on his arms. Did I try to kiss him? Oh, my God. She will never forgive me. I wouldn't forgive me either.

I groan out loud and it sounds strange in the empty house.

I try to piece together what happened but the gears of my brain grind to a stop. My head feels thick as glue. I must have fallen asleep with my phone because I find it stuck to my thigh. I prise it away and it leaves an oblong imprint on my skin.

No message from Anna. One from Jess: *g8 nite sry to leave yous. Hope u had a HBD. Xxxxx*

I need to pee.

A car pulls up outside. I hear the door slam and Dad's voice, then another car door. Strange. He never brought his mates home before. A bird calls out an alarm near my window. The front door shuts. I feel the house rattle.

I hear a woman's voice. 'You could get some help,' wafts up the stairs as they pass through the hallway into the kitchen. I hear Dad's deeper tones, but can't make out his reply.

I am wide awake now and my heart is drumming like I've been running.

Dad thinks I am at Anna's. He's been out all night somewhere – at this woman's? Have they been sleeping together? I want to see her. Mum has been dead only four months.

I get up and grab some clean clothes from a heap I threw on my dresser the other day: jeans, T-shirt, sweater, socks and pants.

Dad's feet bump bump bump up the stairs. 'Yeah, help yourself. Won't be a minute,' he calls down.

He goes to the bathroom, then to his room. I

push my door wide. His bedroom door is open and he is half undressed, changing into shorts and a T-shirt. The swing of the door catches his eye and he looks up. His eyes widen with shock.

'Oh my God, Kay, you frightened the life out of me!' He attempts a smile then brushes his hand across his face. 'I thought you were staying at Anna's.'

'Who's downstairs?' I demand.

He bends down to tie his shoelaces. Give himself a few seconds to think.

'Just Sally from work. Why didn't you go to Anna's?' He's trying to change the subject, but I am not having it.

'Were you at her house last night?'

He walks over to me, his arms open and palms toward me. 'She's a friend, Kay. That's all. Come down and say hello,' he says softly.

'Just a friend!' I snort. 'As if.' I turn my head away.

'Look…' Dad brushes his face again, impatience edging his words now. 'I don't have to run everything by you, you know. I am an adult.'

'Mum's only been dead four months. Forgotten?' I raise my voice, but I can't look at him, afraid to see his response, what might be the truth.

I run down the stairs and stalk past the slim blonde standing by the window in our lounge. She stares, my 'I Love Dogs' cup in her hand, a curl of steam rising upwards. Dad stamps down the stairs. I root for my trainers and pull them on, grab a coat and open the door.

'Kay!' Dad calls, exasperated, concerned. I shrug off his hand.

'Piss off,' I spit and I'm gone. There is only one place I am heading – up the mountain.

CHAPTER TEN

I half-run with a stitch until the house is out of sight. Dad doesn't follow. He's probably sitting on our sofa, being consoled, her arm round him, while she whispers soothing words to ease the pain of his terrible daughter. They will both think, but they won't dare say, how much easier it would be if I wasn't here.

The sky is full of high, racing clouds that cover the sun. The sharp wind seems to clean everything, sniffing through my hastily thrown-on clothes, scouting out to the horizon. I can see for miles. Almost over to the coast and the wet, lapping line of the ocean.

I walk through my stitch without stopping. It feels good to have a clear point of pain, instead of all the thick woolly rage in my head. I am so angry. I am livid. I want to break and hit and scream. Everything that matters is gone. Mum is gone. Dad has already moved on. I have no one. Even Anna is gone now.

I climb over the gate into the field. I want to see the farmer. I want to fight.

The wind flickers the grass. The light hurts my eyes. I walk up and up, curling round the mountain. There are patches of boggy land, puddles and tussocks of grass in between the rocks. It takes concentration not to trip.

Then I notice her.

It is hard to tell her colour with the light behind her. She is trying to lift her front leg, but it's tied or caught on something. I step over to her slowly.

She is a bay. Her eyes are wide and the whites are showing, giving her a mad look. She breathes hard and pulls her leg, trying to retreat from me. Some old barbed wire grips her lower leg and knee joint. Every time she pulls, it digs into her, fresh blood oozing over dried blood. She must have been here ages. The wire is attached to an old fence post buried in the grass. The pony has scraped a fair amount of skin off her leg, probably from straining to escape.

I notice the rest of the herd a distance away. The grey has her head raised and ears pointing high, watching us. The wind laps at me all the time as I scratch my head, pushing the hair from my face.

'Easy, girl,' I croon, edging towards the injured bay. As I creep closer, she snorts and tries to rear. The barbed-wire manacle holds her tight.

'OK, OK.'

I hold my hands up and stop. She is breathing heavily. I wonder about going to get Dad. He would know what to do.

The fury surges back into my heart, throat. No. No Dad.

I don't want to panic her even more. I should go to the farm. The farmer, Croaker, would surely want to know one of his animals was injured? Or is this his barbed wire? I could phone the RSPCA. I pull my phone out: *no service.*

I stumble back the way I came, hoping to get a signal, when I see a figure on the track that belts the base of the mountain. I am sure it is Siôn.

I run towards him calling, 'Hello, helloo!' He is wearing one of those green farmer coats, with the enormous pockets. It is open at the front and the wind pushes it out like wings.

'Hey stop, stopppp!!' I yell as I race up behind him. 'One of the ponies,' I pant as I reach him, 'one of your ponies is hurt.'

He still walks on. Has he got earphones on or something?

I run in front of him so he is forced to halt. Our eyes lock together for a moment that fills out with the wind.

'A bay one, she's got her foot stuck in some wire.'

'Where?' A small crease appears between his eyebrows, as he searches behind me, the hard flank of the mountain.

'I'll show you. Come on.'

I talk while we clamber side by side, explaining what I've seen, until his silence infects me and I stop. He takes furtive glances at me under his mop of hair. His shyness makes a rush of heat creep up my throat. I am very aware of my unwashed face and unbrushed hair.

As we see her, he speeds up and reaches her side. I watch as he mutters to her and glides his palm down her neck. She shows no fear of him, but her nostrils are pulling in and pushing air out in quick little spurts. She lets him reach down and loosen the cruel wire. He hoops it away from her leg, throws it to the side and kneels, examining her knee. She allows him to flex her leg. He stands quickly and pats her once more on the neck. She turns away from him and limps down the hill toward the herd. He begins to make his way back to the track.

'Is she going to be OK? Will you get the vet?' I run after him.

'What?' He looks at me directly, brushing the hair out of his eyes.

'Will she need a vet?'

'No.'

'But won't she need something for the cuts. They might get infected. And she is limping.'

'I'll get some antiseptic from the farm if—' He stops himself and glances down to the farm and then at his feet. 'If I can.' He begins to walk again.

'Can I help? I can hold her or something while you put the stuff on?' I follow him.

'I don't need any help.'

'Well, can I watch then?'

He shrugs. We bound down over the tussocks and stones in silence. I know I don't want to leave him yet. I have nowhere to go.

He halts, gripping my arm and bending low, pulling me down with him. I nearly topple into the wet mulch, but his hand steadies me. He looks out over the tall spikes of bleached grass into the white, open sky. I try to follow his gaze, work out what on earth he's looking at.

'Peewits. They're choosing mates now.'

I can't see anything except the blank white of the sky. But I begin to hear a call, a high whistle that goes up at the end. He smiles at me, a wide, untroubled smile, and I grin back.

'Peewits,' I say, still smiling.

'He sings to her. *Pee-wit*. And he dances in the air too, well, that's what it looks like. A bit like a roller coaster on wings.'

I can feel the pressure fading, where he pressed his fingers against my coat.

A white-and-black bird comes into view, looping the loop. It swoops low, almost into a crash dive, but then pulls up high and begins to zigzag, wings flapping left, right, then left again. Another bird with a similar white tummy flies in and joins the zigzag path. Up they go, high into the white sky canvas. They are so close to each other, it's like they are joined by invisible wires. But then they part and swoop away and out of sight.

As they depart, his face tenses again. 'They'll make nests here soon.'

'They're beautiful to watch,' I agree. Anna would laugh at me, fancying a birdwatcher. But the thought doesn't make me smile.

We walk in silence, listening to the sound of our feet on the track, the crunch of the stones, the squelch of the mud, the *brush brush* of grass against our trainers. I enjoy it, having someone next to me. Not having to talk all the time. I have to stride to keep up with him.

'What's your name?'

'Siôn.'

'I'm Kayleigh. Kay.'

He glances at me, a quick smile. 'You told me last night.'

I remember then, him near our house. Walking in the dark. I feel shame prickle as bits of memory surface – badgers, him at my gate.

'When the peewits have babies, I can show you the nest, but you have to be careful. Otherwise the parents won't come back and then the babies will die.' He smiles again.

I feel my face opening up. It's simple, like the changes in the weather. The sun comes over his face in that smile and brightens me.

'You can't come to the farm. If my dad's there…' he pauses, a frown clouding his brow. I wonder if he is remembering the day with the car. 'He doesn't like visitors,' he adds.

We reach a drystone wall barring the way to the farm buildings. From this distance, they look dark and damp, the roof pitted with broken and missing slates. The paint is almost gone on the window frames, the wood has a chewed look. There are carcasses of cars, drums, the moulding remains of a hay bale, a caravan with blacked-out windows and two dogs on chains, slumped among the weeds. There is no Land Rover.

'Wait here,' Siôn commands. He swings open a small, rusted garden gate, out of place in the gritstone wall. The dogs hear the squeak and clang and start a throat-grating uproar of barking. Their chains chink and scrape on the cobbles.

Siôn lopes down the incline. First he goes to the dogs, whose ears he curls and smooths. They quieten at his touch, their tails beating furiously. Secondly he heads over to the largest building. The entrance is hidden from my view. Moments pass. The dogs watch the house too, sitting on their haunches expectantly.

The door bangs once more and they leap up, straining the chains and nosing at Siôn's pockets. He flings a handful of food down, which they scrabble over, then he strides toward me, some rags in one hand and a bottle of a pink liquid in the other.

'Your dad out then?'

'Yeah, lucky.' A shy look at me.

We begin a steeper ascent up the mountain, off the beaten track, through the mat-grass. There is no sign of the peewits now. The sky looks heavier and I can feel the odd spit of rain on my face.

I want to ask him if his dad has ever hit him again. To apologise for, I don't know what – seeing it, perhaps, not doing anything about it. It hangs between us. I look at his high cheekbone, as though the punch might have left a permanent tattoo, but there is only the natural tones of his skin.

'Doesn't he like you having friends around?'

'Nobody comes round,' he says. 'Well, just some of the men. Sometimes they do work for him. From the village.'

'My dad's always on at me to bring my friends over, but I don't want to. I hate our house. I don't want them to see it.' I feel rage, but it subsides quickly.

We can see the herd a few hundred yards in the distance. Siôn's pace slows and I follow his lead.

'Is your mum gone too?' I ask him, a raw flush of embarrassment on my cheeks.

Again the quick sideways glance, our eyes meeting, his dark brown eyes, expressive.

'Yeah, she's gone.' He tries to smile again, but it falters. He looks lost, like I am; I see all my loneliness, all my aching, wanting, needing, reflected right back at me in that face. Siôn folds his arms tight round him like he's cold.

'Mine too.'

And because there are no sympathetic-pitying looks, no glad-it's-happened-to-you-and-not-me looks, no hope-you-don't-fall-apart-in-front-of-me looks, I can say it. 'My mum died in January...' is as far as I get before my eyes scour with tears.

'I know.'

My throat aches with holding the sound in. I turn away from him.

His palm touches my shoulder, and somehow I am against him, the soft cotton of his T-shirt, a smell of grass and him, the warm knot of his arm as he holds me to him. It is brief, seconds, and we simultaneously pull apart, surprised at the intimacy; so out of place between strangers. I put my hands over my eyes and rub at the tears. Get a grip!

His hand takes mine, wet and cold, and he pulls at my fingers, moving us on, up to the ponies. I follow.

He keeps hold of my hand as we walk closer and closer to the herd. His fingers are warm and dry. I can feel their rough ridges. I feel like the world has shifted slightly, even though the mountain still looks the same, the sky a little darker now, the wind tugging at my hair.

The injured pony is on the far side of the group. The bolder, grey one is looking at us. There seem to be more of them than before. I count ten in two rough groups close by, bays and dun-coloured, and one black one.

Siôn makes a soft noise in his throat, a kind of

whinny. It makes me grin, but he is concentrating. He drops my hand and motions me to stay where I am. He moves closer to the injured one.

She puts her head low and whinnies softly, blowing air out through her lips. She nuzzles at his pocket and he pulls out a slice of white bread that she manoeuvres into her mouth. The other horses are interested now too. Siôn beckons me to follow.

The grey bends her head to me and I smooth her neck, feeling her breath on me as I pass.

'Here.' Siôn gives me a couple of slices of bread. 'Feed her while I'm doing this, keep her mind off it.'

I take them and break off a piece for the injured bay. 'Here, girl, what's this?'

She starts, neighing and pulling, as Siôn applies some of the pink stuff to her cuts, but I stroke her neck and push the bread to her lips. Her ears are back and her breathing is coming fast, but the temptation of the bread is too much and she focuses her attention on me.

The rain begins properly now, fat drops finding the earth.

'That's it,' I encourage her, as she lips the bread and devours it. 'Want some more?'

Siôn is fast and once he has cleaned the wounds with the antiseptic, he wraps the cloth around her leg and ties it. The pony has come to the end of her bread and as Siôn stands to stroke her, making the same soft noise, she nuzzles his pockets. He hands her another slice of bread. 'Last one.' She gazes at him with big trusting eyes, still chewing.

'She'll be OK now,' he says as the herd's heads drop back down to eat, their ears twitching with the rain. 'Come on, I know where we can shelter.' Siôn hunches up his shoulders and runs, turning to me with that open face, to see if I am following.

I hesitate. *Stranger danger, Kay, stranger danger:* Dad's voice in my head. My hand feels cold now he is not holding it. What am I doing?

He stops, watching me. Rain is trickling down my hair, behind my ears and into my collar…

I run to catch up as the heavens open.

CHAPTER ELEVEN

Beyond the gate, the track, Hagg Farm, far from Blackmoss Lane, on the way out to the true moors, there is a dip in the side of the mountain, a mini-valley where a few ancient hawthorns have grown humpbacks. A piece of black polythene has stuck in one of the spiked branches and billows out like a mad crow. The trees nestle round the remains of a stone building. Brown corrugated sheets overlap to make a precarious roof. Eyeless windows and a dark doorway make me nervous. Tall nettles and grass grow around it like a skirt, but across the doorway they've been flattened down – someone has been here already.

We run inside. I am so cold now. The floor is uneven, scattered with large stones where an inner wall must have tumbled down. Siôn sits on one and wipes his face with the back of his hand. Then he smiles. His smile is so unexpected and so artless, I can't think what I was afraid of. He shakes his head like a dog, showering drops about him.

I must have shivered because he says, 'Cold? I'll set a fire.' The rain on the corrugated roof is like hammers. I can hardly hear him. He fetches some dried twigs from the corner. There is a fireplace and a chimney still in place, where a fire has been lit recently. I like watching him, the way he moves about, cleverly building a pyramid of sticks and paper and lighting them with a match from one of his enormous pockets.

'This place is great,' I yell over the rhythmic, battering noise. 'It's like a proper house.'

'It was an old farm cottage. No one's lived in it for years,' he shouts.

Some wooden joists stick out of the wall where a second floor must have been. A green light filters in through the ivy-covered spaces in the roof and the windows. Strange shapes stick out of the grass – a rusty spring, some kind of pan. I pick at the grass that winds about its belly, as though trying to drag it deeper into the earth. Eventually I get it free. It's an old kettle. It has a large handle hanging off at one end.

'Fancy a brew?!' I lift it high to show him and see woodlice hurrying across the base. I drop it in surprise.

Siôn picks it up and turns it over in his hands. Soot rims his nails. He brushes the earth off the kettle and puts it next to the fireplace.

'Just need some cups and we're sorted,' I say, coming to the hearth. Already the fire is crackling and spitting, throwing a warm light into the green gloom. He alternates between warming his hands and feeding wood into the flames. The noise has settled now to a steady pattering.

'Do you want to change? I've got some stuff over there.' He points to the corner, the driest, I guess, where some of the old roof still holds strong. Inside a musty plastic bag, there's a sleeping bag, an ancient Adidas T-shirt and a blue hoody. And some spiders. I shake them off, then check the sleeves to make sure I got them all.

'Don't you want it?' I hold up the hoody, but he shakes his head.

I pull off my coat, one of those thin useless 'raincoats' that soak up water like paper. My jumper is sopping too, all round the arms and the neck. My T-shirt is a bit damp. He is looking at me and I'm pretending I haven't noticed. I pull the cool fabric over my head. I can smell him. It is too big but I can pull my hands right inside and knuckle a fist of jumper to warm my fingers.

'Hungry?' Siôn holds out a packet of crisps he has produced from somewhere, probably his enormous coat.

'Thanks.' I am starving.

He takes his coat off and lays it against a stone to dry a little. It's as though he has taken off a disguise. The shapeless green farmer's skin is discarded, and he looks like a normal boy again. I could imagine him with a drink in his hand, on the edge of Jess's group at a bar, nice gear on, chatting. He sits by the fire. I lean against the wall, feeling the warmth through my damp trousers.

There is space next to him on the stone, but I daren't sit. Even from here I can sense his body: the flex of his arm muscles as he moves; his jaw as he eats, the firelight pinking his skin; the wet slick of his rain-drenched hair; the curve of him, the weight of him. I feel immobile, afraid even to shift my weight to the other foot, drawing attention to my legs, my arms, my body. I realise I am holding my breath.

Siôn seems absorbed by the fire, relaxed and content. I breathe out and tell myself to relax. I am safe here. He isn't going to jump me, force me to do anything.

He breaks the silence in the end.

'So why were you sitting in the ditch at three in

the morning?'There is the hint of a grin at the corner of his mouth.

It is my turn to shrug. 'Bad night.'

'Bad?' He looks up at me, expressive again, interested.

'I fell out with my best friend. My fault. I'm a silly bitch sometimes.' I pick at the grime under my nail.

'Don't call yourself that.'

'What? Bitch?'

'Dad always used to call Mam that. I hate it. You shouldn't call yourself that.'

'Is that why she left?'

He shrugs and half nods, stares into the fire.

'Is this your escape then?' I ask, shifting my footing.

'I just visit here sometimes.'

'Does your dad come up here?'

'No, he's never up on the mountain, except to get the ponies.'

'What does he do, ride them or something?'

Siôn spits his crisp out as he snorts. 'He doesn't ride.' He looks at the fire. 'He sells them.'

'Oh, right.' I try to sound as though I understand. 'I've always been a bit afraid of horses, but your ones don't scare me. Especially the grey one. What's she called?'

That shrug again. 'They don't really have names.' He hunches closer to the fire.

'Hey, we should do this place up. It can be a proper den. I used to have a den when I was a kid, in the field behind our old house.'

'A den?' He is back with me again, smiling. He shifts over to make room for me to sit.

'Yeah. Me and Anna used to camp in there and once we found a dead cat in the field.' I make a sick-face.

'Don't you like dead things?'

'I remember it got smaller and smaller all winter until you could see the bones sticking through its fur and once she dared me and I went right up to it and it had no eyes, just like dark spaces. Yuk.'

He makes a spooky face at me, daft like the boys at school, and then–

'I've got almost a whole skeleton of a rabbit and loads of skulls: a sheep one, a fox, a horse.'

'You're joking?!' I exclaim. 'Why? That's just weird!'

'No.' He shuts up his face, gazing away, lips pressed.

I wish I hadn't used that word. It hangs awkwardly in the air. He is strange, but he is not weird. He feels more real than anyone else right now, as though the rest of my life is just a dream.

'I mean, I don't think *you're* weird. I just–'

He shrugs. 'There's nothing to be afraid of.' He has a patient look on his face. 'They're just bones. It's fascinating, how different they are, and you can tell the size of the brains from how big the cavity is. And they feel so smooth and cold.'

'Don't they smell? I mean, aren't they dirty?' I remember the matted black carcass of the poor cat, things crawling in it, on it, decaying. Death.

'I don't collect them till they've been dead a long time. They're all clean. Some of them are beautiful.'

I can't keep the distaste off my face.

'How can you live if you are so afraid of what's under your skin?' he says matter-of-factly.

'I'm not afraid.' I feel myself pout, the stubborn face that always made Mum roll her eyes. 'It's just most people don't have a collection of skulls in their bedroom.'

Siôn reaches over and stokes the fire a little, sending sparks up. 'How do you know I keep them in my bedroom?'

I make the face again.

The rain has almost stopped now. I am thinking I should go when he says, 'Fancy a game of cards?' He pulls a pack of ordinary playing cards from his coat, shuffling deftly, one way, then the other. 'What do you want to play? Rummy? Pontoon?'

'I only know how to play Snap,' I admit.

'Snap?!' A grin peels across his face and then we are both laughing. 'OK. Snap first, then I'll teach you Pontoon.' He edges along to make room for me to sit, for us to play. Our knees touch gently and I see him shift his weight away from me to avoid it. He probably doesn't like me that way after all. I feel relief and disappointment collide.

The tension evaporates as we play fast and furious, our fingers brushing as we rush to be the first to snap. I am winning for the second time when the violent blast of a gun in the valley fills the air and makes us both pause. I can hear birds cawing anxiously. Another blast.

'I'm going to have to go.' Siôn drops his cards to the floor and throws his coat over his shoulder.

'Oh, OK.' I pick the cards up. 'Wait for me!'

He is already out of the door. I leave the cards in an untidy pile on the stone and trip out after him.

'You'd better go a different way. He's home. I don't want him to see you.'

We hurry our way through the humps of grass. The rain has stopped now.

'Why? I'm not afraid.'

'It's just better if he doesn't know anything about you.'

He pauses suddenly. My arms jerk forward to stop me from falling into him, but instead I catch him. His face is right in mine. I can see the Marmite colour of his eyes, the honey flecks. He looks so lost. I can't help but touch the smooth, healed cheek with my fingers.

He kisses me. My eyes are open and I see the olive blink of his eyelids, then his gaze refocuses.

'He has a habit of destroying beautiful things,' he says quietly, almost pushing me from him.

'Do you – will you be up here again?' I call, as he swerves down and away from me.

'Yeah, come to the den,' he shouts over his shoulder.

He uses my word: den. 'When?'

He can't hear me.

I scramble higher, pulling myself up on the tufts of sturdy grass, finding gaps in the stones and the heather, until there is no view of the track or the farm below. Simply me and the sky.

The sun splits the clouds again and I hear the 'peewit peewit' call. He just kissed me, this odd guy, with his collection of bones and enormous coat. I laugh as I imagine Anna's face if I could tell her about Siôn. I breathe in the cold, high, grassy scent. None of the rest of it matters.

I make my way home, glad to feel the wind drop as the mountain curves toward the lane. I am spent now. I feel clean inside, like the wind has blown away every bad part of me, all the thoughts and feelings that have been thick inside me, weighing me down and slowing me up. All I feel is excitement, like light exploding, my head full of Siôn.

CHAPTER TWELVE

It isn't until I am climbing over the gate, walking up to the house, my steps reverberating up my legs, that my stomach snakes with anxiety. Dad's car is outside and the door is unlocked. But there is no sign of him. I have four missed calls from *Dad*. I creep up the stairs into the bathroom where I have a long shower. My skin prickles with the heat. I am tired. And starving. I've been out most of the day. I rub the shampoo into my scalp, loving the warm silkiness of it, my eyes closed, feeling light clouds of suds cascade over my shoulders, across my breasts and down my spine.

I wonder what Siôn meant by saying his dad destroys beautiful things? Maybe because of his mum.

I wonder what the gunshots meant. I wish I could talk to Mum about it all, or Anna.

After I've changed, towel-drying my hair, I pad

down into the kitchen to get something to eat. Dad is sitting at the island reading his paper. He doesn't look up. I feel my lips tighten as I think of that woman and I can't speak. I take out the bread, open the drawer to get the bread knife and slide it closed with a bump. I carve the bread in the silence.

'You're making a right pig's ear of that loaf, Kay. Here.' Dad's chair squeaks as he stands and his cool, sandpapery hands take the knife. He cuts two straight pieces and throws the lump I cut in the bin.

'Oh, don't throw it away. I can take it for the horses.' I pull it out of the bin's swinging mouth.

'Is that where you have been all day?' Dad switches the kettle on. 'You must tell me where you are going, Kay. I was worried. It's after six.'

I root around in the fridge for cheese. Spilled milk stains have turned sour. I shut the door.

'It's private property up there,' Dad continues his lecture. 'You've seen what Croaker is like.' He bends his head and sighs. 'Look, I'm sorry about bringing Sally here. I know it's too soon. I only came to get changed as we were going for a jog. I wouldn't have brought her if I'd known you were here, love.'

He gazes at me, sincere and imploring.

'Is she your girlfriend?'

'No, no. It's difficult to explain.'

'You slept together last night,' I say, exasperated.

'I slept at her house, yes, but nothing happened.' He stirs the milk into my tea, just how I like it.

'I don't want her to come here,' I say quietly.

'OK. OK. Look, I love your Mum. I always will. I miss her too.'

His eyes fill up and he crushes me in a hug. It feels so strange being comforted by Dad. He is so bristly, there is no softness, and a zip from his top sticks into my cheek. I let myself be hugged, knowing he means it. The phone rings and he lets go self-consciously.

His side of the conversation isn't terribly revealing, so I finish my cheese on toast. When he returns, his face has a guarded look.

'Anna's mum,' he says. 'She says you have left some things at her house.'

My stuff is there, I remember, and so is the expensive present they bought me. My guilt returns full force.

'Will you get them, Dad? Please.'

'We'll go together.'

On the drive over to Anna's we don't talk much. Dad doesn't ask what happened, but I know he is thinking about it. When we pull up outside her house, I look at him. 'Please will you get them?'

Dad purses his lips. 'I think you ought to face whatever it is, Kay. It will be better if you do.'

I get out and slam the door. He winds down his window. 'Sorry is always a good place to start.'

Bloody useless stupid advice I didn't ask for.

I go up to the door and knock. The dogs go mad barking. Anna's mum comes, my bag and the gift in her hands.

'Hi,' I say, as she opens the door fully.

'Hi, Kay.'

'Is Anna there?'

'Yep. One moment. Anna!' her mum calls over her shoulder. She doesn't make way to let me in and I know Anna has told her it was all my fault. Bloody Joe.

Anna won't come to the door. We wait in awkward silence. 'She must have slipped out, Kay love.' She smiles at me sadly and hands me my things.

I hesitate as she passes over the gift, that someone has placed carefully back into its wrapping. I don't feel I should take it, but Anna's mum pushes it firmly towards me and lets go, so I am forced to hold it.

'It's yours,' she says.

I feel tears begin to brim up. 'Will you tell her I'm sorry?' I whisper as I step away from the door, clutching my bag and the present.

'Give her a few days, she'll come round.' Anna's mum moves forward slightly, as though to hug me, but then she steps inside. She raises her hand goodbye and shuts the door. I walk back to Dad. Perhaps I should write Anna a letter, like we used to do when we were younger, written in code so her brothers couldn't read them.

Dad is hulked over the steering wheel, preoccupied. 'Did you sort it?'

'Yep, everything's fine.'

CHAPTER THIRTEEN

On Sunday, Dad insists on taking me out for a meal for my birthday. Theresa meets us at the pub and talks at us for two hours, while I try to stop myself yawning. I want to go to the den. I'm not sure if Siôn is real or if I imagined him. By the time we get home, it is pouring with rain. I don't see how I can get away without Dad noticing. The last thing I want is him following me and ruining things. I don't want to wait, but I have to.

After I say goodnight to Dad, I go upstairs to text Anna, telling her how sorry I am for being such a complete bitch on Friday night. I sit down at my desk under the skylight. I haven't drawn the blind down and the black square of night keeps catching my eye, like a dark pool. Everything is so quiet. I can't even hear the TV. There is no noise of cars or passers-by. My desk is the one tidy place in the whole room. It is decorated with bits I've collected: a fuzzy sticker we were given at a careers fair with school; a postcard from Theresa from Venice; a picture of us girls last *Children in Need* day, all wearing pyjamas in class. Anna has her arm round me. Jess is the other side with her tongue out. I didn't even know Mum was ill when that picture was taken.

I don't know what to message. I don't fancy Joe, but I am jealous all the same. I remember what he said, *You don't like me being with her…* He is right. I don't like it one bit. She is my friend. I need her.

I ramble on about how drunk I was and how Joe wound me up. I say how sorry I am, how afraid I am of losing her. I say it is no excuse and that I can't blame her for hating me, but if she can forgive me, I'll never drink again. Blah blah blah.

When I have finished, all I can think of is how unfair it is. This fist of rage grips my chest. Anna has known me forever, Joe only five minutes, but she won't hear my side of the story. I look over the text, all sorries and let's be friends, and I press delete, watch the blinking cursor gobble up my words one by one until there is no message left to send.

I have kept Siôn's jumper; it reminds me of him. It is nothing special. No marks or labels, just an old chewed pull-cord in the hood that I twist in my fingers until finally I fall asleep.

I wake early. I wonder what time Siôn wakes up. Is he down at the badger set, or up watching the peewits, with the fresh wind blowing the sleep away? I am so tempted to walk up to the den and wait for him, but Dad offers me a lift to school. I don't like him coming to the school with his copper's uniform on, but it is still early so I don't think many people will see.

'Hope it all goes OK today,' he says, as he pulls to a halt by the railings. I roll my eyes and he pats my arm. 'You'll be fine.'

The tutor lets me into our form room, with raised eyebrows at my being first in. I avoid a conversation by sticking my head into my school bag, and looking at all the stuff I haven't done. It is a welcome distraction, something different to worry about. When she arrives, another girl in our class, Vicki, lets me copy her notes from History.

The room fills up and the bell goes. Still no Anna. Jess is talking about the bloke she met on my birthday, oblivious of anything else. Then I see Anna's blue top through the gap in the door. She sits in her normal seat next to me and I breathe for what feels like the first time since I arrived at school. She doesn't talk to me or look at me, but at least she's there.

The day drags. First break is pretty awful. Anna is

in a different Maths group to me, so by the time she comes into the café, Joe has his arm round her. He has obviously been forgiven then. He glowers in my direction and takes her off to sit with his mates. I want to smack him one. It makes me so annoyed; I go out and mooch round the library with the Year Sevens, pretending I'm looking for something.

The library window faces out over the car park, and beyond to Blackmoss and Foulstone Moor. Being with Siôn, having that warmth, company, even for a little while, and for it to be gone again, makes the loneliness even colder. The bell goes.

It's English. We are asked to do some pair work revising the characters in *Romeo and Juliet*. Anna scrapes her chair back and goes over to the teacher's desk. There is a glance over to me. The teacher nods his head. Anna moves to sit with someone else, and I am left on my own.

Everyone's eyes are on me.

I know they are talking about me. It is always me and Anna. Always. My eyes travel over the lines in my book, a highlighter in one hand, but nothing makes sense.

When we are packing up, as the high-pitched squeal of the bell sounds, I go over to her. 'Can I talk to you?'

'What?' She stuffs her folder into her bag and rummages around for her phone.

'About Saturday. It's not what you think.' I can sense other people in the room listening in, but I don't care.

She shuts up her face, just as she shuts up her bag. 'Joe said you'd say that.'

Anger explodes within me. 'Well, he would. He was as much to blame as me, winding me up. I didn't mean to tell him what you told me, about–'

She snorts and wraps her arms tighter round herself. The last of the class drift away from us and out to next lesson.

'I was drunk. Look, I'm sorry.'

'You're always drunk these days.' She turns to go.

'I didn't kiss him. I don't like him.'

She pauses and without turning round says, 'He said you'd say that too.'

I can't believe she won't hear me. She believes him over me. I am so fuming. I grasp her arm.

'Anna! So – you're just going to take his side, your *boyfriend* of two weeks, over me? I thought we were friends.'

'So did I. I don't know you anymore, Kayleigh.' She shrugs my arm off. 'You're always pissed, and you're always–'

'Always what?' I reach for her again, with more

force this time, but she pulls away, and as she does so, she loses her grip on her phone.

There is a moment's pause as I watch its arc. Anna makes a lunge to grab it before it smacks against the door handle. Too late. We both hear the crack. It lands face up, the screen a web of shattered lines.

She picks it up and storms away.

It is easy to dodge school at lunchtime. I sign myself out and just don't go back. The sky is clear and the wind quite warm. The bus rumbles out of Beesley, gradually getting emptier as I get nearer home. I feel sleepy, my arm in a patch of sun in the window. If anyone says anything, I'll just say I was sick.

The walk up the lane wakes me up again. Dad is still at work so I change quickly, grab Siôn's jumper and some scraps I've been saving for the horses, then jog up the lane toward the PRIVATE sign on the gate. I pause to retrieve the rucksack I hid behind the wall. The whisky is still inside in the coke bottle.

I'm not always drunk, I think. Anyway, Anna would need something too, if her mum had died. No, her life is perfect. It is me who's got no one. I shake the grass off the bag, and a couple of stray spiders, then carry on.

I scramble up the hill so fast I am out of breath and sweating. Every step away from the house, I feel better, liberated.

'Here, girls. Here. What's this?' I call to the mountain, hoping to see the shapes of the ponies picking their way toward me. I keep walking until I can spot them in the distance, oblivious to me. They are too close to the track and the farmhouse for my liking, but I scramble down to them, calling gently.

Eventually the grey sees me and begins to amble over. I can count only five. The one with the bad leg isn't there. I frown. I wonder if Siôn's dad has decided to take her to the vet after all.

The air smells fresh. Spring is bounding toward summer, and the new growth, the bright smears of grass and some spots of purple in the heather make me smile.

The ponies reach me and the grey noses the bread bag in my hand.

'Hey, how are you?' I whisper, stroking her neck as she munches on some bread, her ears flicking lazily about. 'Where's your mate gone? Hey?'

The other four crowd in when they realise food is on offer and I hand round the bread and apple cores, trying to be fair.

Suddenly their ears prick. They stand taller and

begin to trot away, up the hill. The grey stays with me but she neighs. My heart beats faster.

A voice shouts. I turn. Mr Croaker is storming up from the farm, a barking dog at his heel. He climbs over the stile, still roaring at me.

I panic. I think of the gunshots and Dad's warnings. What Siôn said. Will he shoot me for being on his land?

The white pony nuzzles me, fitting her nose under my elbow and lifting it. The fast drum roll in my chest makes me move. He is a hundred yards away and will be on me in seconds. I shift the rucksack onto my shoulders.

'What the fuck do you think you're playing at, EH? EH? YOU. I'M TALKING TO YOU.'

I know how to do this. It's one of the tricks we learned riding, though then I had a step to stand on. Luckily the pony is a small breed, and panic gives me power. I thread my fingers into the pony's mane and lift my right leg over her back. Pushing with my left foot, I manage to get astride her. As though she's been waiting for me to do this, she canters nimbly after the other ponies, who are out of sight already.

I can feel her muscles moving through my thighs. Afraid of slipping off her smooth back, I clutch on with my knees like we were taught to do, and lean forward into her neck, locking my fingers together.

'Good girl,' I call. 'Good girl.'

She breaks into a gallop and leaves Croaker standing, his hands on his fat hips. His dog chases us, but only half-heartedly, rounding to its master, barking and baring its teeth to us.

I can't help laughing. I am riding! The jolting is terrifying and makes me whoop. Any moment I could slip and fall under her crushing hooves. She is smooth like tight velvet, but firm too, with little to grip on to. The pony's heat melts into my skin as I try to bounce in time with her. The breeze unpins my coat and billows up my spine. My elbows jolt and my teeth knock.

We loop round the wide base of the mountain where I've never been before. The track is gone. She slows down, much to my relief. I am rigid from clinging to her. Her muscles ripple under my thighs and I shift my weight in rhythm. It is like the movement of a boat, but warm, firm and reassuring.

Croaker is long out of sight.

My pony joins her herd, hesitates at a broken wall and stands still.

'Thank you, thank you,' I murmur, smoothing the pony's ruffled neck. I dare to sit up straight and stretch. 'What can I call you?'

The bright white horizon gleams and the coarse grass ripples in all directions. Foulstone Moor. In the distance, the tor rises, the great slab of stone where we threw Mum's ashes into this space.

She munches at a patch of something more edible between the mat-grass. I swing my leg over and lower myself until my feet are on the ground. My legs are jellified and untrustworthy, so I lean against her flank, picking at the mud and bits that are knotted into her coat.

'Sky. I'll call you Sky.'

The rest of the herd are moving away, unruffled, as though nothing has happened. As I sit on the grass, Sky comes to me and breathes warmth into my hair. And then she moves away too.

CHAPTER FOURTEEN

It's a lot trickier than I thought to get to the den. The ground is boggy in places, rutted, with tussocks and stones hidden under the long mat-grass. I nearly twist my ankle more than once. It's harder to navigate than I expected, with no buildings or trees to guide me. I climb over the wall and head up the mountain, but from this angle I can't remember if it is further to the right, or towards home, higher up, or if I have missed it.

Eventually I see the few trees able to grow up here, and I drop down into the little dell, a bit more protected from the wind.

The building stands waiting for someone, its blank, glassless eyes seeing nothing. I pause to listen. There are no noises, but then a peewit starts its call in the distance and I feel reassured.

The gloom inside is the same as before, still and

empty. It smells grassy and of old leaves. Siôn must have been here because someone's made a shelf from a slat of wood and two bricks. The playing cards have been collected together and stacked on it, next to a book about birds, *The Encyclopedia of Birds of Britain and Europe, Mountain and Moorland.* He has left it open on the page about the peewit.

I smile. He is real. I take bits I have brought out of the rucksack, putting the coke-with-whisky bottle on the little shelf, then I settle down on a stone to read.

Abundant in marshes, meadows, moors and fields. Easily identified by long thin crest, black and white colour pattern. Wing beats rather slow and in breeding season the erratic display flight is conspicuous.

It's a library book, long since out of date. I flick through the pictures of all the different birds. It's cold without Siôn's nice little fire, so I walk about to warm up and see if there is anything else to find.

There's a noise outside. My heart skittles in my chest. I shrink into the corner, feeling the granite rub of the stone against my fingers. The door opens and a cool light blossoms in. I can't breathe, imagining Croaker, his mouth wide with roaring.

It's Siôn. He looks bigger than I remember, taller, as he stoops slightly to enter under the old stone lintel. He has his old coat on. I take in the brown skin of his neck, his dark hair.

'Hey.'

It's his turn to start. He swings round and drops the bundle he's carrying. 'Jesus!'

I start to laugh. 'You scared the life out of me too!'

He smiles. I feel embarrassed. He looks pleased I'm here.

'Look what I got!' he says, lifting something out of the bundle and unfolding an old khaki camping chair with a rusty metal frame.

'I thought they'd been chucked but they were in the back of one of the sheds.'

'Handy.' I smile, coming closer to help him. My fingers brush against his waxy coat as I pick up a second chair.

'We can be comfier now,' he says.

I try to unfold the one in my hands, but it is stiff from lack of use.

'Here,' he offers, holding out his hands.

'I can do it.' I tug at the rusty metal. It pulls apart, wafting a damp smell into the air that reminds me of camping.

He puts them next to each other by the fireplace and grins at me. We sit side by side. I swing my legs. Siôn is close. I feel alert to his every movement, even the rise and fall of his T-shirt as he breathes. His hand rests on the arm of his chair, millimetres from mine.

'Have you just seen your dad?' I ask, picking at the fraying material of the chair.

'No.'

'Oh.' I look away. I want to grin as the memory of riding Sky washes over me, the exhilaration of the escape.

'Why?'

'I saw him earlier.'

Siôn's face darkens and his eyes flicker to the door.

My smile fades. 'He wasn't here. It was by the track.'

His hands link together briefly, away from mine.

I shouldn't have ridden Sky. Will things be worse for Siôn because I did?

'I could meet you on the lane next time—' Concern frames his features.

'I like coming here,' I say quietly.

The ivy is flickering in the window space like a green curtain. I move closer to look outside. A fresh wind tugs at the grasses and the sun blinks in and out of the clouds. I feel sad, the rush of excitement at seeing Siôn ebbing away. There is a gap, a cave in the centre of me once more. I wish I had a drink – a can of Dad's Stella, WKD, the whisky I brought, anything to make me feel better.

'Well, you've got to come and see the badgers. The cubs are getting bolder all the time now.'

I smile.

'You'll have to wear something warm. I usually go about eight-ish, when it's going dark. If it's windy we can't go, because if they catch our scent they won't come out.'

I focus again on what he is saying. His matter-of-fact tone. Arranging to meet again. He does like me.

I kick at some mud on the edge of my trainer. Meeting him again, at night – the rush begins flooding back.

'You could text me,' I say.

Siôn shakes his head. 'No phone.'

'Oh.' I feel stupid. Of course the normal ways I would communicate with a friend wouldn't work with Siôn. There are no phones. There is only us, up close to each other.

'I normally go on Thursdays, unless the weather's too bad.'

'OK.'

'So if it's windy or raining we won't go.'

'OK.'

'But otherwise…' Siôn breaks off.

'I'll meet you at the bottom of the lane.' I am grinning now. 'I'll tell Dad I'm going to Anna's. He doesn't need to know I'm with – a boy. He'll only moan at me.' I try to make my gaze mild. I cannot read his expression.

'Comfy,' he says, copying me and swinging his legs on his chair.

And we are both laughing, but I'm not really sure why.

CHAPTER FIFTEEN

The sky is a deep navy, lighter out beyond Beesley, where faint snakes of cloud still reflect a hint of the day's warmth. The air is cool and still, full of grass and damp wood smells. Colour is draining out of the day, the field green turning to grey. I can still see though, still make out the individual branches in the different trees.

'Here,' Siôn says in a low voice, pointing to a gap in the hedge. We're at the edge of the wood. He pushes his hair out of his face. 'We can't talk after this. They are used to me now, but we don't want to scare them.'

I nod and grin. He smiles back. He holds the brambles out of my way as I dip under to enter the darkening wood. Even though I sneaked a can of Dad's beer before I came, a flutter of anxiety prickles my stomach. How dark will it get?

There's enough gloomy light here to see a way. Grass has been trodden in a thin path through the slim trees. As we go deeper in, the trees are bigger and further apart, with small clearings where the grass is long and the sky makes shapes in the branches.

We don't go much further before Siôn halts, listening. I can hear nothing except my own breathing. He starts walking again, slowly, then he stops. I see the shape of a fallen tree, shadows blooming underneath it.

'I need to put the torch out,' he whispers. 'Stay here.'

He leaves me stooping behind the wet bark of the dead tree. It smells of mould and feels slimy. I put my hands in my pockets.

Siôn walks quietly around the edge of the clearing. He lays his torch on a raised grass hummock and switches it on. A pool of yellow brightness throws the shadows into deeper blackness. There are no badgers, but I can see Siôn's face in the glow of light, as he wends his way back and crouches next to me.

'Very David Attenborough,' I whisper. Light flickers in the dark pools of his eyes as he smiles.

We wait. I can see the shapes of the trees, the dark blue of the sky above us, the varying greys of the ground.

'Won't the light scare them?' I breathe.

'Normally it would, but these're used to it. Get comfy, it might be a while yet.'

My legs start to ache. I wonder what Anna is doing, how she would laugh if I told her about this. I can't share it with her now though, can I? And I don't want to share it with anyone else. They'd just take the piss. I look at Siôn's face, intent and earnest, as he watches the clearing without blinking, his eyebrows raised, boyish. Those others don't know anything.

A movement in the grass makes Siôn straighten up. We both watch the space beyond the pool of torchlight, where a dark snouty shape appears. A badger pauses and sniffs, then comes forward and stands, listening. She is bigger than I imagined. I thought they were a bit like cats. She is more the size of a dog, but low to the ground.

Siôn grins at me. I am grinning too. She has the strong black-and-white markings across her face and a little fat tail. She starts to root about in the grass, moving further away from the sett entrance, every now and then pausing and looking about her, sniffing, listening. Another stripy face appears – a smaller badger scurries out, no caution at all. And right behind him two more, all snuffling about. The bigger one I guess must be Mum. She moves out of the pool of torchlight, but the three cubs stay close to the sett. The first one makes a funny growling noise and begins to bite the tail of one of the other cubs. He rolls onto his back and kicks at his sibling with his back paws. They break apart and carry on foraging.

Siôn pats my arm. I have been too busy watching the mischievous pair. I didn't notice the third little one, who is just an arm's length away now. I can hear her snuffling noises and see the reflection of light in her black eyes. I want to reach out and touch her, stroke her, feel her warmth.

Siôn's face is alight, all the weight and brooding gone from his eyes. He loves them. He laughs quietly as they tussle and chase each other.

We watch them for ages, as they feed and play about. It's mesmerising to be so close to these wild, beautiful animals. Eventually they follow the path their mum took out of the clearing. I move my legs, aching all over from staying in one position for so long. I realise how dark it has become. The light from the torch seems to be waning too, unless it's just my imagination.

Siôn creeps over to reach the torch and as he picks it up, the light disappears and I am plunged into darkness. My stomach dips and I clench the rotten bark of the tree trunk to steady myself. I feel the graze of his coat against mine.

'Did you like them?' he asks quietly, as we begin to weave our way back through the wood. He puts his arm around my waist and gives me a squeeze. It feels as natural as the woods, and warmth breaks through the dark coldness in my chest.

'They're amazing.'

My feet feel the firm earth and the thin, whispery grass bending under my shoes. Siôn's arm leaves me. I can see brief glimpses of grass and bark and the rest is blackness, threatening to swallow us completely.

'Are the batteries going?'

He bangs the torch. It makes a half-hearted attempt to shine, but the light is even more feeble than before.

He laughs. 'Looks like it.'

I say nothing, not wanting to sound weak and stupid. I try to stay close to him without making a fuss.

But I can't stop the fear rising. Fallen branches and tall grasses make traps for my feet. My heart starts to run ahead of itself and my breath is high in my throat. It's only the wood, I tell myself. The dark cannot suffocate me.

'Siôn?'

'You OK?' He turns to me. The light from the torch is useless now. It shows only a glimmer of his hand. Above us, the black of the trees and the lighter black of the sky. 'I know the way, without a torch. It's OK.'

There is nothing there in the wood, just empty shadows, owls and foxes and the badgers. I know it, but the fingers of the dark seem to be pulling at me. I take a deep breath in, smelling the wood, damp and old leaves. But still the darkness loops inside me, clogging up my lungs.

I stumble and grasp out, catching hold of Siôn's coat.

'I can't breathe.'

He holds me to him. His fingers lattice with mine, the grain of his skin firm and warm. My heart is loud in my ears. I close my fingers tight against his. I am not letting go.

He leads me out into the field, a breeze, stars and shadows.

'Are you all right?' he asks, when we are safe back on the road by the neat street lamps with their acid light.

'I don't know.' I kneel down. The smooth grey pavement feels so good I could lie down, put my cheek against it and go to sleep. Maybe I could sleep here without dreams, without nightmares.

Siôn rubs my back slowly. Like Mum used to do.

'I've had it before, when it is really dark. Like I can't breathe.'

'Why didn't you tell me? I could've brought a spare torch.' He sits on the pavement next to me.

I shrug. 'I don't like it. Being afraid.' I look at him and my eyes begin to fill with tears. 'There's nothing else that can happen to me now. I shouldn't be afraid.'

'Everyone's afraid of something.'

'No. You're only afraid if you care. I am not going to care about anything.' Anger makes me sit up and glare at him.

He holds my gaze. 'I don't think you are the kind of girl who doesn't care.'

'I don't want to care, ever again. Not for anything or anyone. You don't know,' I say, standing up and crossing the road.

I head back into the black night of Blackmoss Lane. I know it and I dare the fear to come. Angry tears burn my cheeks. I will not feel. I will not love. I will not lose anything ever again.

The fear does not come, because there is a faint light from the village, a faint glow from our one street lamp. I hear Siôn's steps behind me. He doesn't speak, but he stays with me until we are close to my house.

'Kay,' he says.

I stop and wipe my face with the sleeve of my

coat. He comes up to me, blocking the view of the village below us. I will not look at him. I can't.

He puts his hand under my chin and lifts my face. 'I know,' he says. 'I do know.'

He kisses me, on the lips, and he holds me fast, knitting me back into a person again with his warmth. Dad's cough inside the house brings me back to the present. Siôn steps back silently and with a wave of his hand, he slips into the night.

CHAPTER SIXTEEN

The next day it is raining, so there's no trip to find Siôn. It's a crap day and I am getting further and further behind with school. All the teachers keep saying things like, *'It's not like you, Kayleigh,'* when I get another E in a mock test, trying to pry to find out what's the matter. Though it's pretty bloody obvious. The only decent one is my Art teacher, Mrs Strong. She says it doesn't matter what grades I get, I can always resit *'at a better time.'* She knows without me saying how bad things are. How I just don't care anymore about exams and grades and all that.

When I return from school, on the doorstep is a small clean bone. It looks like a triangular boat, with a small ivory sail. At first I think next door's cat has left it. I pick it up and smooth it under my thumb like a shell or a stone. It is delicate and a creamy white, but too clean to be a recent kill. I notice next door's curtains swish into place.

Anna has completely frozen me out. She won't sit next to me in lessons, and whenever I join a conversation, she walks off. I'm hanging around more and more with Jess and her lot, but there's always some drama with them. I feel invisible. It is Thursday and it is Art. There is some athletics trip on, so hardly anyone is in. I sit in my usual place; Anna sits by the window. Mrs Strong makes us all a brew, then gets us all round one table to look at this artist's work that she saw at the weekend. There is a book open on a large image of a face in black and white. It looks as though it's been scraped sideways, as though an invisible hand is pulling the skin off. There are some postcards too, all with the same kind of scraped and distorted faces.

'What does it make you think of?' Mrs Strong asks as we stare at the pictures on the table.

One kid picks up a postcard. 'Looks like he lost the fight with a paintbrush.'

Mrs Strong smiles. 'Anna?'

Anna purses her lips. She hates being asked questions in class. 'They look really – painful.' She smiles apologetically.

'Good. Yes. There is a lot of pain here–' Mrs

Strong rambles on about Auerbach and his dead parents, then sends us to carry on with our portfolios.

'Another happy artist.' I perch on a stool at Anna's table.

She pulls the lid off her sharpie with a click.

'Did you get your phone fixed?'

'Do you need to sit here?' She looks me right in the eye. Cold.

I stare at her. She really is going to do this. Throw away our friendship. All the years of it. I want to bite back, but I hesitate; I feel like I am dissolving.

She sighs and places her palms on the desk, looking at me. 'It's not always about you, Kay. Not everything is about you.'

'What does that mean?'

'You are not the only one who has problems, Kay, that's all. I can't do this.'

She gives me this look, squeezing her eyes, the pupils bright and shining. She stands up, squeaking the legs of her chair.

'What do you mean?' I ask again, but she is walking out of the class.

The bell hasn't gone yet. Mrs Strong stares at her disappearing back, eyebrows raised over her glasses. She looks at me for explanation.

I know I'm not the only one to have problems. I

know that. What is Anna's big deal? She doesn't know she is born. Maybe she has found me out, sussed out my secret – my need for her, so vast and wide and desperate. I feel ashamed, like I have let the cover slip and shown my true and terrible self.

But the truth is even worse. The person I really need is dead. What am I supposed to do with that?

Mrs Strong comes over. 'That isn't like Anna, to walk out.'

'No.' I start to stuff my things into my bag.

'What you are going through, Kay,' she sighs, 'it's incredibly tough.' She takes off her glasses and rubs her eyes with her thumb and forefinger. 'Losing your mum. It's too tough for some people to manage.'

I stare at her, unable to put any of it into words. She replaces her glasses. 'If you need anyone to talk to…'

'I'm OK.' I shift my bag onto my shoulder.

'You are dealing with it magnificently, but, well, you don't have to hold it together all the time. This door's always open.' She smiles. My cue to escape.

'Thanks. I'm fine, but thanks though.' I walk away, feeling her eyes on me all the way.

Dealing with it magnificently? Oh my God. The woman knows nothing. It has been four months and I still wake up aching for Mum. Dad is moving on.

And Anna. I am so cross with her. I know it was me in the wrong, but I expected lovely Anna to forgive me. Why has she thrown away our friendship over a boy, a few drunken words?

Well, I've had it. I'm done with Anna and I'm done with school.

It is raining when I get home, and a downpour by the time I reach the den. There is no sign of Sky or Siôn. My disappointment sits heavy in my stomach.

Brushing away some of the ash from the last fire, I ball up some pages of *The Sun* that Siôn brought and make a wigwam of sticks, just like he does. There are hardly any matches left in the battered box, but I light the paper on the second time. It burns quickly, coating me in its friendly orange light, but the sticks don't catch and once the paper's all gone, the fire is just cold black ash. I try again, but I can't get the sticks to burn.

I sip some of the flat whisky and coke, still in its bottle on the shelf.

I am freezing.

I am not capable like Siôn. I don't belong anywhere. I'm not part of my old life, and I am useless at this new one. I know I have to go home. I promise myself tomorrow I will come back prepared. I will come to stay.

As I walk home, the rain making my clothes heavy, my jeans sticking to my thighs, my ears stretch for sounds. I haven't seen Croaker since I rode Sky. Occasionally the dogs bark, but they are far down at the farm.

Nothing.

Eventually I have to drop down to the gate. The light is starting to go, and house lights are blinking on in the valley. I check no one is in sight before I slip and skid down to the gate.

But someone else has been here since I stormed through this afternoon. New silvery barbed wire snakes around the gatepost, tightly wound so there is nowhere I can put my hand safely. Strings of spiked wire cross the top of the gate too. Is it a trap? Is Croaker watching me?

I will have to get over one of the unkempt walls. I scramble along the drystone wall that separates Croaker's land from the gentler fields beyond. I must be able to get over somehow.

Skirting up, up the mountain, as the darkness comes, there are no breaks in the defence. Eventually I reach a lower point – it's the best I can do. The wall is about as high as me. I manage to find some footholds and scramble up. The stones rock as I put my weight on them. Desperation makes me bold and

I leap from the top, grazing my hand on a hidden boulder when I land.

I stumble down the steep field, tripping once and bashing my thigh on something I can't see, then rolling down the bank. 'Ow!' I come to a stop, lying in the short, nibbled grass, looking up at the blueberry-coloured sky.

I sit up, rubbing my wrist. I can dimly make out the lighter shapes of sheep, who avoid me, bulking together and moving into the gloom. Staggering to a stand, a sharp sensation burns in my thigh as I walk. I don't want to look. The darker wall-shape lines the lane home. The gate to this field has not been wrapped with steel thorns, and is easy to climb, despite my throbbing leg.

My feet hit the tarmac of Blackmoss Lane and relief floods through me. I hurry as fast as I can back to the lights of home, trying to ignore the ripping pain. I am so glad to shut the front door behind me, feel the centrally-heated warmth and smell some cooking smells. I hear Dad swearing in the kitchen.

'Christ, Kay, what happened to you?'

I look down at myself. I am soaked to the skin and covered in mud. I have scratches on my hands and my trousers are torn and bloody. My leg is killing.

'I forgot the time and it was a bit hard to see the way.' I untie my laces and unpeel my dirty gear.

'I told you to tell me where you are going.' He bends down to inspect my leg.

'It's fine, I'll sort it.' I dodge past him to the stairs. He huffs but doesn't follow me.

I lock the bathroom door and pull off my trousers, chucking them straight in the bin. My leg is worse than I thought and I feel a bit sick looking at it. I make myself inspect the gouge between my knee and my groin.

'Dad, Dad!' I call down the stairs.

A curved shard of glass about the size of my thumb is stuck in the wound, hard and glittering.

He has to take me to the hospital in the end. The nurse uses tweezer-thingies to pull it out. She lifts it up and shows it to me. 'Part of a bottle,' she grins. 'Another reason we shouldn't drop litter.' She is one of those women who think all kids are the same, blaming us for the world and all its problems. I won't smile back. Her and Dad bond over my accident, while she cleans the wound and gives me a couple of butterfly stitches. I am a bit light-headed and dizzy, and happy to zone out of their conversation.

'You're lucky, it's quite superficial,' she says in that

tone of voice again. 'Maybe teach you to be a bit more careful next time.' She helps me sit up.

Dad snorts. 'There won't be a next time, will there, Kay?' He pretends to be all in charge and I glower at him.

On the way home in the car, I am feeling sleepy with the heater on. I quite like the sore point of pain in my leg. It feels like a focus and leaves the rest of me free to forget. My whole body is beginning to ache.

'I don't feel very well.'

Dad frowns at me. 'Well, what did you expect?'

I shrug and close my eyes. He is very quiet. Occasionally he mutters something to himself under his breath. I wonder if he should be driving as I can smell the drink on him.

When we stop the car, I go to take off my belt and he turns to me.

'I mean it, Kay, you're not to go up there anymore. It's not safe.'

'Up where?'

'You know exactly where, up to Croaker's place.'

'It was an accident and it wasn't at Croaker's,' I argue, which is true.

'Well, wherever,' he says, not to be side-tracked. He sighs. 'I am not asking you, Kay, I am telling you.'

Which makes me laugh. As if Dad can make me do anything. He has never bothered before and it is too late now. I can see it in his face: he isn't sure of himself and the words sound hollow, his voice tinny and far away.

'I don't want you going up there anymore. And you shouldn't be drinking either,' he says, gripping the wheel resolutely. 'I know you took the whisky. Christ, Kay, you're only sixteen. I don't know what's got into you.'

I snort. 'Don't know what's got into me?' I splutter. 'God, you're such a hypocrite. You drink, why shouldn't I? I've got more reason than you.'

Slamming the car door petulantly, I storm up to my room. He won't come up here. I put on some tunes, loud enough to annoy him. I dare him to get me to turn it down. I want another fight with him. I want to tell him what a crap dad he is, how crap my life is, exactly what has *got into me*. Prick.

But he doesn't come. Eventually I calm down and turn the music off. I am knackered. I only want to sleep.

Why couldn't I have seen Siôn? Next time I will take a torch and stay there all night to wait for him. That will show Dad.

I am stuck in bed for two days. Some kind of flu,

Dad reckons, because I got so cold. He wants me to go back to the doc to check I have no infection in the 'wound'. But he can't make me, so I don't. It doesn't stop raining the whole time. My sleep is fitful and I dream bitter dreams, of wild horses and men with snarling dogs.

I wonder if Siôn has been looking for me.

CHAPTER SEVENTEEN

Pringles. Galaxy. Some fruit. Bread for the ponies. A bottle of cola. A travel sleeping bag. Torch. Lighter. Book. Wipes. I don't need my bloody phone. I put on as many jumpers as I can and set off up the lane.

I expect to have to climb over the wall again as the gate is now impossible. But when I get there, the padlock is unlocked, threaded through the chain. Is this a sign Siôn is expecting me? I unhook the lock and weave the chain out. It clanks loudly, and the gate screeches on its hinges as I open it, making my heart begin its one-two one-two march. I dip through as quick as I can and put the lock and chain back, all the time listening for the Land Rover, ready to run. Then I am up into the long grasses and the boulders, away from the track and heading for the den.

I can't see the ponies. I wonder if they are stuck

on the wrong side of the wall. The sky is white with cloud, but still bright enough to hurt my eyes and make me squint. I can see for a long way, over the farm and beyond. The wind, never still up here, tugs idly at the grass. Nuggets of sheep poo lie among the scrub, or maybe it's rabbits'. Something else living up here, free and alone, away from the world. I never want to go home. Dad would be all right after a bit; school would be glad probably. I wouldn't fail my exams and make them look bad.

I am almost at the den when I hear a whinny of recognition and see Sky trotting to greet me.

'Hello, lovely.' I stroke her as she bends her head to trouble the rucksack, hunting out the food.

'OK, OK, here.' I pass her an apple, which she bites into and then drops, the juice seeping out over her lips in frothy delight. She nuzzles it on the ground then lips it into her mouth.

'Where are the others?' The rest are nowhere to be seen. 'Just you, eh?'

Sky nuzzles under my elbow again as though she wants us to ride. 'OK,' I say, 'not too fast this time though, Mrs.'

I heave the rucksack onto my shoulders and climb onto her back. She trots along, her ears pricked and alert. There is no way to steer her and I do not want to go too far from the den and have another accident. 'Come on, girl. Enough now. Enough.'

She whinnies and turns sharply. I am not expecting it and almost lose my grip. Then she is cantering and I am bouncing and clinging on for dear life. She heads to the den. And then I see why. Siôn is walking towards us up the hill, making a loud clicking noise with his tongue.

He is missing the great lumbering coat today, and only has a T-shirt on. His arms swing loosely as he clambers up to us. He looks younger and more carefree, his hair brushing away from his eyes in the quiet breeze.

Sky brings herself to a halt next to him. I try to look cool and in control and sit up straight, my fingers threaded into her white, straggly mane. 'Hey!' I grin widely, shifting my weight in turn with Sky as she bobs after the bread Siôn hands her. He is frowning.

'What the hell you doing up there? It's not safe.' He makes to hold Sky's mane and take hold of my hand. He does not look at me, keeping eye contact with the pony instead.

'It's OK. She's a good girl. Why are you cross?'

'Come on, come down.' He tries to help me off her, but I am annoyed and shrug off his hand, landing lightly on my feet.

'You don't need to fuss. It's not the first time we've been riding, is it, Sky?' I pat her neck and smooth her nose.

'No, I hear,' Siôn says grimly, giving me a glance for the first time.

'If it wasn't for Sky, your dad would've fed me to his dog, I reckon,' I try to joke.

Siôn says nothing, stroking Sky in long rhythmic movements. Then he slaps her rump and she snorts, trotting off a few yards.

'Come on.' He takes my hand and leads me into the den. He already has a fire going and there are more books on his little shelf. The bottle of whisky is still there too.

'You not cross with me now?' I ask him.

'I wasn't cross. Worried.'

'Sorry. It just makes me feel so free.' I grin and raise my arms to the roof.

'Don't get too carried away,' he says, touching me lightly, both palms against my sides. We are up close and then, aware of it, we move apart, embarrassed.

'Where are the other ponies?' I don't like to think of Sky on her own. She seemed so strong before, leading the others, and now she seems small, skittering over the mountain alone; a needle slipping through the grasses.

'You shouldn't give her a name. She isn't a pet.'

'Well, I have. She comes to me when she sees me now.'

'You shouldn't get too attached.' He is exasperated, but milder.

'There's no harm. I know she doesn't belong to me. Don't worry.'

'It isn't that. I just don't want you to get hurt. Riding. My dad. These ponies aren't meant for pets. They won't be here for long.'

'Why, where do they go?' I move toward the fire to warm my hands.

'Get sold.' He changes the subject. 'I wanted to come over on Monday, but Dad kept me busy all day. He even made me help with wiring the gate up. Said we have trespassers after the horses.'

'Look what I did to my leg.' I roll up my trousers and hitch them as high as I can above the knee. He can see the curved scab and the stitches. I can smell his fresh, salt smell as his head bends over my knee. He touches it gently with his forefinger. His palm strokes my skin around the wound, leaving trails of nerves prickling.

'That's not from the wire, that.' He sits back and looks at me.

'No, glass. Probably a bottle. I did it falling over

the wall to get home.' I let go of my trousers and they fall back into place.

'I couldn't loose the padlock that day, but I have tried to every day since, just in case you could make it.'

'I couldn't walk too good the first couple of days, but it's not hurting much now.' I smile at him. 'Did your dad say he'd seen me on Sk – the pony?'

'Mmm. He's been trying to catch her since, but she's too clever for him.'

'What will he do to her?'

'Sell her on.' He stands to get more wood. 'He is going to anyway. But he hates anyone enjoying themselves so he wants to do it now.'

I watch him as he moves across to collect a bunch of firewood. The light is tinged with green from the ivy filtering the daylight, and warmed by the fire.

'I didn't know if you'd come today. I bought a torch and my sleeping bag. I'm not going home,' I say.

'You're mad.' He laughs out loud.

I shrug, trying not to smile. 'Well, I just wanted to get away, to see you. I hate my life.' I fling an arm in the direction of the door. 'You know, out there.'

He grins like a little kid. 'Me too.'

'Hey, have you drunk that whisky? Or shall we have some?' I need a drink.

'Is that what's in it?'

'Didn't you taste it?'

'No.'

I take it from the makeshift shelf and open the top. I sniff. It is strong. I decant some of the fresh coke into the bottle and take a swig. He sits on a low stone with his elbows balancing on his knees as I make a lemon face and thrust the bottle at him.

He shakes his head.

'No?' I ask, having finally swallowed.

'No, thanks. I don't drink alcohol.' He is watching me curiously.

No, of course he doesn't drink. He is the badger boy, my mountain boy, all clean and pure and weathered. He belongs out here, like some wild creature. He isn't part of the foul, ugly life I come from. I swig some more. I need it. To forget myself.

'Why do you drink it?' he asks.

'You're different.' I try to explain. 'Most of us at our school, we all do it. And weed, and some of them try cocaine if they can get it. Not me. But this is, well, just what you do, isn't it, to relax. I suppose.'

'My dad's always drunk. Doesn't make him relax.' Siôn stretches his arms up, making his torso elongate, and then settles back again.

'No?'

He shakes his head.

'You don't mind if I –?' I hold up the bottle.

'Depends how you act when you're drunk,' he says seriously.

'I don't get aggressive, if that's what you mean. It makes me more confident.'

'Do you need to be more confident?'

We are trying to read each other. I watch him, trying to work out if he is being fake coy or if he really doesn't know: his skin, the way it glints in the firelight and the smooth hairs on his forearms, the ruts of bone on his fine powerful wrists, his hands. I remember how they felt. I twist my fingers together to make a lattice, a net about the bottle.

I take another swig. 'So what's your dad like when he's pissed?'

Siôn stares into the flames as though far away. Then he shakes his head slightly. 'Mum says he'd fight his own shadow.' He sighs. 'It makes him worse than normal.'

'Worse?'

'Yeah, a worse bastard.'

I swallow the sickly medicine of whisky and coke.

'Is that why your mum–?' I ask.

Siôn nods. 'Did you find the rabbit bone I left you?'

I fish it out of my pocket and hold it up to the light. He looks pleased.

'It's a shoulder blade. I found it here at the den ages ago. Do you like it?'

How can you like a bone? I hold it in my palm as the firelight plays across the smooth surfaces. If you don't know what it is, it is like a small sculpture, crafted and honed.

'It is beautiful.' I place it carefully on the shelf.

'The peewits have got a nest now. Soon I'll be able to show you the eggs. You'll like them too; though we can't touch them. I'll get you a shell when the babies hatch.'

I smile. There is a silence. I take some more whisky and feel bolder.

'So, where is your mum now?'

Siôn shrugged. 'Probably gone to Nain and Taid's.'

'Who?'

'My gran and grandad's. They live in south Wales.'

'Why didn't you go with her?'

Siôn stands up and stretches again. 'This is my home. He should've gone, not us.' There is a pause. He stands over the fire, stretches again, and when his arms come down to his sides, he looks different, sort of mischievous. 'Can I see what you look like without your clothes on?'

His face is dark against the firelight, and I can see the mercury pools of his eyes glinting.

'What? Now?'

He nods, watching me, his head cocked slightly to the side. 'I've never been with a girl,' he says.

I try to look calm but my heart's drum is echoing round my body. I don't know who to be. I need the drunken me, but she's an actress late for her cue. This is just me. Plain old me. No clue how to act or what to do.

He sits down next to me. I can feel the heat off his T-shirt from the fire. He doesn't touch.

'Most lads – don't usually – just ask like that; they sort of build up to it.'

'Oh.'

Then he kisses me. He puts his palms either side of my face and presses his lips hard against mine. My stomach makes a little twist. He pulls away and keeps his hands on my cheeks, threaded into my hair, his index fingers soft against my ear lobes. He meets my eyes. I try to make mine bold, wanting, fake eyes. Not terrified.

He kisses me again – the same hard, bumping kiss, our teeth almost knocking together. I lean back and kiss his lips more softly, but he pushes his tongue into my mouth and I am saturated with something

I've never felt before, overwhelmed with it; he is pressing against me and my body is responding. It is a weird feeling, a kind of melting hunger, a wanting to mould into him. I pull away this time, panting slightly. I feel afraid, but I'm buzzing all over.

Siôn gets the sleeping bag and lays it out in front of the fire, then he takes my hand. His warm hand in mine. I unpeel my jumpers, my T-shirt, feeling the goosebumps ripple over my flesh. There is nowhere to hide. I unhook my bra and lie down on my front. The cool nylon of the sleeping bag feels silky. One half of my body floods with heat from the fire and the other is tight against the cold. I close my eyes.

He lies next to me. I hear his short breaths. I feel his fingers connect with the skin at the nape of my neck, their roughness down the line of my spine.

'Nice shoulder blades,' he says quietly.

I open my eyes and see his face close up, the black eyelashes down, the lick of his eyelid. 'I hope you aren't planning on adding me to your collection.'

He grins. I close my eyes again, hardly breathing. Waiting. Any moment.

'Turn over,' he says.

I keep my eyes tight shut as I shift my weight toward the fire and then lie down feeling the slippery shift of the sleeping bag under my skin. Now the cold side of me is warming and the warm side protests at the withdrawal of heat.

I want to see him looking at me, but I stay here behind the lids of my eyes. Separate. I feel his breath on my skin.

His fingers trace a line from my throat down to the button of my trousers, and up again. Then his fingers stop. There is a pause and I think I might pass out. I feel the warmth of his lips on my skin, an explosion of sensation. I arch my back slightly. He stops.

I open my eyes to see him lying next to me on his back, staring at the sky through the gaps in the rusty corrugated iron. He is breathing heavily. I lie there too, returning, back to the den, to myself. I look at him now.

I trace his profile with my finger, along his throat, down his chest, seeing the bruises on his arms, the cuts on his forearms, a scar dissecting his collarbone. He brushes at my hand and grips it in his.

'Too ticklish.'

He leans over me, one leg caught into mine. We are kissing, his hands on me, my back, my neck, in my hair. I feel him against my thigh and my heart is overwound, doing double time.

And then I'm gone. I am still kissing and my

hands are still moving, but I feel mechanical. The only real thing is the tick-tick tick-tick.

Panic rises in my throat, but I'm not sure what to say. Messages crowd in at once: *What are you playing at? Just get on with it. Not pissed enough? You've led him on, you can't stop now, this is why you're here, isn't it? This is all you're good for...*

I am no actress today and the tears begin.

'I can't.'

He doesn't hear. Why doesn't he hear me? His hands are pulling down my pants and I can feel him loosening himself out of his jeans.

'Stop.' I push at his arms. He grins as though it is a game. Then he sees I am crying. I wrap my arms about my legs, my breasts tight to myself.

He stands up, paces up and down by the wall, his hands over his ears. Then he grabs his T-shirt and leaves. My eyes black out against my knees.

I hold myself to myself, the only thing I have left. I pull the sleeping bag over my bare skin and lie there, until gradually the crying stops. I sniff and quieten. And breathe.

I can hear him, by the door. I do not turn my head, but I hear him moving toward me and I hold myself rigid again.

'Did I hurt you? Sorry. I'm sorry.' He bends and

draws a strand of hair away from my face, smoothing it down.

I shake my head.

He passes me my T-shirt and I put it on, hooking my bra on underneath, embarrassed.

I say, 'Is this all ... is that why? Just sex?' Another tear leaks out, across my nose and drips.

'What?' He strokes my hair.

'I thought you liked me,' I croak out, rubbing my face into the crook of my arm.

'I do.'

'But ... why is it just sex? Always sex. I wanted you to hold me. I thought you understood. I just wanted – I don't know.'

'You don't fancy me.' His hand moves from my hair and he sits on his heels, still close, just behind me.

'But I do. I just–'

'Hey, it doesn't matter. It's OK.'

I turn to him and he holds me and I cry and cry and cry.

'The fire's nearly out.' I say, looking up at him, at the glowing embers, and wiping my face.

'Yeah, I'll get some more wood in a minute. You OK now?'

Siôn disappears outside. He is gone some time. I feel better. Calmer. I sit watching the last embers, poking at them with a twig and then dropping it into the ashes. It is getting dark outside.

'This should do it.' Siôn plonks a few fresh twigs on the fire, but they are a bit damp from yesterday's rain and won't light.

I look at him in the gloom. 'Sorry. I got a bit freaked out back there.'

'Why?'

I shrug. 'Scared.'

'Me too.' He moves next to me, holds my hand tight in his two palms. I put my head on his shoulder and we sit there for a while not saying anything.

'I should probably go home. I don't want Dad sending out a search party.'

'Yeah. I'll see you to the gate.' He stands and pulls me up, wrapping his arms round me. I hug his chest.

'You're cold.'

'Nah, I never feel the cold,' he says.

We walk without a torch, taking our time. It is a clear night, no moon, just a few stars and the leftovers of a sunset on the horizon. I have all my jumpers on, but it takes me a lot of tramping over the tussocks before I am warm again.

'I'll come tomorrow. If you want,' I falter.

'Course I do,' Siôn replies.

'I'll bring a picnic if it's nice. I want to climb to the top.' I gesture with my head to the peak of the mountain, now in blackness.

'Sounds good.'

'Do you go to college, or anything?' I realise I still don't know.

'No.'

'Well, I haven't got school tomorrow either,' I lie, 'so I'll be up in the morning, if you like.'

'I'll keep an eye out. But watch out for my Dad.'

'Always.'

I kiss him, a warm, dry goodbye, and we part.

CHAPTER EIGHTEEN

'How many times do I have to ask you to tell me where you're going?' Dad complains when I walk through the door. 'It's nearly ten o'clock. If you think you are getting any allowance this weekend–'

'Finished?' I hang my coat up.

'Not really. There is a call from the school. Apparently you came home at dinner time.'

'I had a headache.'

'You can't walk out without telling people. Anything could have happened.'

'Well, it didn't.' I think of Siôn's weight on me.

'I come home and there's no washing-up done. Your stuff's still wet in the machine–'

'I'm supposed to be revising for my exams, aren't I?'

'Oh, that's a laugh!' He snorts and kicks a dead can of Fosters that he has thrown on the floor. I watch it skitter across the carpet.

There's a heavy silence. He's right, of course, exams have never been further from my mind. He sits down, facing the TV, but not taking any of it in. There is an empty chip-shop packet next to him and another dead can nestled in the debris.

'You don't do anything in this house,' he grumbles.

I roar, 'I'm not picking up after you! I'm not your bloody mother. Mum mothered you and you did nothing to help her. Well, you can piss off if you think I'm taking her place!'

I storm up the stairs. My heart is going again, but this time with rage. I sit on the edge of my bed in the dark.

I'm starving and realise I've left my rucksack in the den with my chocolate supply in it. I don't dare go downstairs.

I never rowed with Dad before Mum died and I'm afraid of how far I can push it. I know I ought to help around the house, yadayada … but I feel this rage, bursting through me. There's nowhere for it to go.

My door doesn't have a lock, so I push a chair under the handle so Dad can't walk in. Everything feels heavy and fierce in my chest.

I think about Siôn's skin. The feel of him against my leg – it floods me with wanting. I climb into bed naked, and my eyes close as I remember him. It isn't long until a moment of pleasure rushes through me, but is quickly gone. I am empty again. Empty of everything: pain, rage, desire. And I can sleep.

'Kay!'

Daylight floods around the edges of the curtains, oozing through the pale material. Dad is banging on my door.

'What you got behind here?' He turns the handle, but the chair stops the door from opening more than a couple of centimetres.

'I've got you a cup of tea. I'll leave it here. Time to get up. Bus goes in an hour.'

'Thanks, Dad,' I yawn.

I get the tea and creep back into the snuggly warmth of the duvet. I feel bad that I rowed with Dad yesterday. I make a half-promise to make more effort, enjoying the tea he has made for me. A flush ripples through me as I remember today's plans. I get up to check. It is a bright day, bit windy, but no rain.

I dress in my school gear. Dad usually leaves before me, which is handy. I am making sandwiches when he comes in to grab his keys.

'No dinner today?' He pauses, watching me carefully, the crease between his eyes deepening.

'Oh, right. No,' I stall, avoiding his gaze. 'We've got a revision trip to the library in town. Healthier than chips,' I lie.

He raises his eyebrows.

'Phone school if you don't believe me!' I bluff.

'OK, but no skiving today, Kay, please.' He kisses me on my head and is gone. It is easier to believe me, less hassle for him.

When I am sure the car engine has faded into the distance, I phone the school number. 'Hi, it's Kayleigh Simmonds. 11H. I won't be in today. I've got a migraine.' I listen as the receptionist explains I need to bring a note from my dad to confirm my absence. Three weeks till we break up, I think, what are they going to do? At least this way they will not phone Dad.

I change quickly and pack the picnic, adding a little extra for Sky. Just out the door, I stop. I run back up the stairs, root about in my top dresser drawer and fish out a condom packet. They were giving them out in Health Ed. a few months ago. The same lesson where we had to peel one over a banana. Yep, still in date. I stick one in my jeans pocket and stuff the rest back.

As I walk up the lane I think about Siôn. I have never felt like this about a lad before, and that makes it harder, not easier to think of having sex with him. The closeness of it, the realness of it, makes me feel nervous-sick. I can't work it out. Planning it seems to make it more embarrassing: the condom, a badge of intent in my pocket. I will not think of it. I am good at that now, putting the difficult things under lockdown. Up here, I can leave all the difficult stuff behind. It is only us and the wind, and Sky.

I hear a sound of a diesel engine, in low gear, coming up the lane. The Land Rover. I can't see Croaker, but he will soon see me, obvious against the weather-bleached tarmac. I need a place to hide. The walls bordering the lane are drystone monstrosities, difficult to climb. A gate about 100 metres on the left is my only chance.

I run fast, legs pumping. The bumblebee sound of the engine grows louder and louder. I crash into the gate and haul myself over, as the Land Rover turns the corner. I am hidden.

I sit, feeling the gritty wall through my jumper, after the drone of the engine has long gone. I almost bottle it, and turn for home. I think of school. I already feel a thousand miles from the place. I know in my stomach I will not go back.

I decide to carry on along this side of the wall, rather than risk the gate. It is hard work but I'm well away from the track here, safe from bumping into Croaker. He doesn't have the physique of a man who does much walking.

Sky meets me and after a snack of carrots, I mount her and trot to the den. The air is full of spring today, warm and light. The dew is still heavy on the grass and the sun reflects each glittering drop. Spiders' webs, knotted into the gorse, shine like tinsel. By the old cottage, bluebells are beginning to flower. I wonder who lived there last and why they left. It's too nice to go inside, so after checking Siôn isn't in, I spread my coat on the ground and sit, leaning against the stone by the door. Sky grazes, gradually wandering out of view. It is the clearest day yet and I can see for miles, the valley beyond flattening out, merging into the grey sprawl of the city.

A peewit starts its call, a shrill warning signal, somewhere out of sight. I glance across and see, among a knot of bramble, a spider balancing in air. I watch as it reaches the far branch and begins to return, knitting together its silver trap. I reach out and touch the filament of light, but the thread breaks. The spider drops, legs frantic to weave a lifeline before it hits the ground. It does. It hangs there, poised, before starting the whole process again.

'Moorland spider. They're really common.'

Siôn's voice makes me start. He moves to stand over me, a shadow against the sun, his T-shirt sleeves exposing his dark arms.

'Hey,' I smile. He takes my hand and helps me to my feet. He's wearing the same gear as yesterday, but he's clean and his hair is still damp from showering. His eyes look warm, relaxed.

'Saw your dad today,' I say, running a hand through my hair. 'Close shave.' I grin. 'He didn't see me.'

'He went into town early.'

Siôn looks at his feet, rubbing a little mud off one trainer with the edge of the other. I lean into him and kiss the edge of his lips. He smiles and his face loses its faraway look. He kisses me back.

'We going to the top today then?' he grins. He takes my hand. We run.

I whoop and pull away from him, struggling to gain a lead. He leaps over a large mound of grass and lands on his knees, then he's up again. I am getting a stitch and laughing at the same time. I have to stop and he overtakes, running backwards and making a face at me. He makes the clicking noise and Sky appears, trotting up to us, her tail swishing.

'There's the remains of an old settlement at the top. Iron Age, they think. No one's ever excavated it. There could be ancient tools and all sorts up there.'

'How far is it?' I look up the steep side above us, all scree and grass. I still can't see the top.

'It's not too far, just a bit steep. Half an hour probably.'

'You know a lot about it up here.'

'I was no good at school so Mum used to teach me at home for a bit. We did loads of stuff about the mountain. I always loved learning about it with her.' He looks up at the high, clear side of rock above us.

'You know loads.'

He shrugs. 'Stuff never stuck in my head at school. Took me ages to read and write and by then I didn't want to go. I did some stupid things so they sent me to Rutherton. But I left last year.'

I remembered Jess's words about the kids in the special school. Dad saying they are always having to call the police in. I can't imagine Siôn stuck in a place like that.

'What do you want to do now you've finished? Run the farm with your dad?'

Siôn snorts. 'There isn't much farm left to run. He's sold nearly all the livestock and the machinery. There's hardly any money. He deals with the horses now, and lets the place fall apart.'

I don't understand why Siôn stays with Croaker. If his mum escaped, surely he can too?

We begin the steeper climb and it gets harder to talk. Sky stands at the edge of the scree and watches us for a while, before turning and taking her own path away from us, among the gentler terrain. The farm is in view again, just a centimetre-square of greyness, of no consequence. You can even see the track, the gate, the lane, my house and its small collection of neighbours. I breathe in deeply; I am far away from it all. If only I could keep walking, never return.

Siôn is in front. He knows the way through the tricky rocks and boulders and I follow his lead. He keeps glancing behind to make sure I am still here, that I am OK. After a time I need a breather, so we stop for a snack, eating the biscuits and drinking some water. Siôn is amused at how organised I've been, though he eats ravenously.

'Didn't you have any breakfast?' I ask, offering him the rest of the packet.

He shakes his head. 'No food in.'

I think of home, the constant palaver with Dad about shopping and what to get and writing lists. I can't imagine Croaker being like that.

'When did she go?'

Siôn frowns at me as he tries to follow my train of thought. Then it clicks. 'Months ago. Last November.' His eyes flick away.

That is our bond: motherless children. All those things our mums have done for so long without us ever realising – the cooking, cleaning, washing, shopping, ironing, caring, loving, giving. And now with the gap, the great aching cave in the centre of my life. All those things she did, who was going to do them now? Me? No way. But somebody has to do it. In a family.

I kick a stone down the scree, watching it skittering and gathering bounce.

I am going to college, university. I am going to have a career. It has always been that way. Until recently.

'You could be a vet, or a scientist. You know so much about animals,' I say, thinking out loud.

Siôn smiles through his biscuit. 'Too stupid.'

'You're not.'

He shrugs, that Siôn way of shaking off the difficult conversation.

'What do you want to do? When you leave?' he asks me.

'I wanted to go to art college. I really like designing stuff, patterns and things.' I sigh. 'Can't imagine it now, though.'

'No?'

'I'm going to fail everything. I've done no work for ages.'

A silence, as we look out over the panorama. The sun is warm but the breeze is cool and I wish I had brought my coat up from the den after all.

'Look!' Siôn takes my arm. He is pointing down to the scree to a gap in the bigger rocks, close to the base of the granite. There is a rabbit, hopping carefully out into the open. She pauses to nibble slim blades of grass growing out of the scree.

Siôn smiles at me. 'C'mon.'

We hold hands as we walk the final stage to the peak. It is the hardest part yet. Scree slips and slithers, threatening to take me with it. I am hot and out of breath. The tops of my thighs ache, and the wound in my leg throbs dully. If Siôn wasn't here, I would probably give up. I want to be like him, still bouncing and energetic.

But then the last boulder is here and there is no more up. We've done it. I've done it.

He grins at me, lifts his arms above his head and yells, 'Wooohooooo!!!!!!!!!!!!!' I grin, sitting on my haunches and catching my breath.

The whole world is laid out in front of us. In every direction, for miles and miles. I can see the greens of the mountain smoothing into the ochres of Foulstone Moor, and on the far horizon, a jagged edge of cliff rising up, like the helm of a ship, angular and dark: Hagger Tor. In another direction is the valley, and the greyness of houses gradually becoming the city. In another direction Hagg Farm, home and school; Anna and Jess and all of that. They all join up. One great enormous picture with us right at the centre, so much space about us, it is as though we are above the sky. I lift my face up into the wind and turn round and round, making myself dizzy. I could lift off and fly.

Siôn grabs me and I swing into his arms.

'We did it!' I grin. His whole face is laughing, even his eyes, and he kisses me. Soft at first and then harder as we press against each other. His T-shirt cool against my hot skin. His skin warm like mine.

We break away, our eyes reading each other. This time there's no fake acting, I am vulnerable and real. All me. And I don't need to think about it. We are on top of the world, after all.

I take his hand and clamber over a wall of one of the old iron age buildings. It is a kind of circular wall with a gap for a door, only as high as my hips, its edges blurred where stones have fallen and others landed. It makes a good windbreak. The sun flickers out and butters our faces.

I kiss Siôn. This moment is all there is.

I take off my own top and unfasten my bra. Then

I pull his T-shirt over his head. He is kissing me and we are holding each other, clinging to each other.

I undo the button of his jeans. My fear is all gone, evaporated into this rush of adrenaline. His hands slide my trousers down and I lean onto a great seat of a boulder, feeling the sandpaper of the granite surface on my skin.

His thighs are against mine, warm and firm, and I feel everything rushing through me like a river from each tingling point of light – the place where my neck meets my collar, the goosebumping of my arms, and down, down.

He is letting me lead. Kissing and nuzzling and holding. My hands fold down the smoothness of his thighs. I want to laugh at us being up here, the cold wind and how hot we are, and then my stomach swoops. He is watching my face and we both have our eyes wide, like oh my God we are going to do this.

I remember, 'The condom, the condom,' and I am laughing as I feel in my pocket, and he holds me and I feel him, dry and hard and warm. I want to touch him.

'I've never put one on before,' he says, and I laugh again because neither have I, and our hands are shaking as I rip the packet and he takes it and we peel the condom on together and then he kisses me and it happens; up there above the world, with the sky so big and bright, connecting us to this great mountain, its roughness, its beauty.

I am fizzing all over. He leans into me, his head on my shoulder, and it isn't fair it has stopped already.

'I haven't come,' I mewl.

His face turns from the nape of my neck. His dark lashes flicker against my skin. 'How do I make you come?' he asks, and I show him how.

After, we are shivering. Freezing. Siôn passes me my jeans, and we balance against each other. I hunker down away from the breeze, inside the walls. Siôn buries the dead condom under a stone, then he nestles down beside me, grabbing my hands and wrapping them in his. I feel like I might fall off the summit and plummet down down down if I don't cling to Siôn like this.

'See?' he says, looking at me sideways.

'See?'

'See.' He is grinning, giggling happily.

'What?' I am grinning too, but I don't know why.

He nudges me with the arm resting against mine.

'You.' And he hugs me tight.

'Me – what?' I stroke his hair away from his face to read his eyes better.

'You are beautiful.' He isn't grinning now. He is looking at me looking at him. And I believe him.

'So are you,' I say.

CHAPTER NINETEEN

'Cold?' Siôn says into my ear. He must have noticed the goosebumps puckering up my arm.

'Mmm.' I nod. 'And hungry.'

'Time to go then.' He pulls me up, keeping hold of my hand.

'To the den?' I ask, afraid of him slipping away from me. I couldn't bear to let go of him right now.

'We can make a fire.'

It is a lovely feeling, coming down the mountain; my muscles are loose as we jump and stumble down the steep scree. Him pulling me, me pulling him, keeping each other from falling. The light is crisp, the horizon far. Hagger Tor and Foulstone Moor disappear from view, and instead the falls and flats of ochre greens and blondes lie in front of us, the small nut of dark that is the farm, still too far away to care about. I look, squinting into the sunlight, but there is no sign of Sky.

We hardly talk at all. Being together is enough. I know him now. This strange, beautiful boy. Almost as though he has become part of me. It's me and Siôn now. Nothing else matters.

'This'll do for the fire.' Siôn pulls at a dead branch of hawthorn curled into an old wall. It is awkward and heavy and he has to drag it, the brittle spikes snagging on the ground.

'I'll help.' I take the weight, but the sharp spines pierce my fingers. 'Ouch, ouch, wait.'

'It's OK, I can do it.' He gives it a heave.

'No.' I tuck my hands in my sleeves and use them like gloves to get a handhold on the sharp wood. Together we carry our firewood down to the den.

Siôn makes the fire, and once it gets going, he breaks up our find into smaller pieces. I watch his strong hands pressing against the brittle wood till it breaks; scratches on his skin. He doesn't even notice. The fire is roaring now. Then he fishes out some sweets he has stashed. I savour the toffee melting sweetness, staving off my hunger for a while longer.

'I'll get the sleeping bag, shall I?' he says, already pulling it up out of the bin bag in the corner and shaking it. He lays it down in front of the fire and dives into it, grinning at me.

'Hey!' I complain. 'Where am I going to go?'

'Come on.' I giggle as he gestures for me to squeeze in next to him. 'There's loads of room.'

He laughs too as I wriggle down into the one-man bag, the zip tight against my tummy. Neither of us can move. I unzip it a little and free my arms, then wriggle about until I have my back to him. He puts his arms round me and puts his face into my hair.

'You OK?' he asks.

'Mmmm, you?'

'Yeah.'

I can feel him the whole length of my body. I close my eyes, too tired to move. I love this. It's like we are Iron Age people up on the mountain. We've got fire, each other. This is our house now and we could live here forever. His arms go heavy and slack and his breathing has changed.

I briefly wonder what we are going to do for tea, but it seems too mundane to think about that sort of thing. Could we live up here, grow vegetables, get a cow…?

I am dreaming when the voice becomes clearer and I wake. The fire is gone and it's darker now. Startled, Siôn is shaking his head and struggling his way out of the bag. His knee brushes against me roughly, and he is on his feet. I look up. His face is caught with terror, eyes blank and small.

'You bloody nag. You can't get away now!' Croaker's harsh voice cuts through the last crumbs of sleep.

Outside, the sound of Sky's high whinnying taughtens my nerves to stinging wires. Siôn runs to the door, but he hesitates, a hand on either side, as though to steady himself, to hold us in. I push past him. I can hear myself yelling, but my voice sounds far away, fragile.

Sky is cornered against the old house. Croaker has a rope halter and his gun under his arm. He sees us out of the corner of his eye, not wanting to take his attention from the pony.

'Siôn, come here and fucking help me now. Siôn!' he roars, spit slipping across his lips. He is trying to get closer to Sky, while keeping his torso and head tilted away to avoid her kicking and rearing. He shifts his gun up with his elbow to keep hold of it.

'I'd fucking shoot you now, but it's too far to drag you. Pain in the bloody arse. Come on, Siôn, or I'll make you carry the carcass back from here.'

Siôn makes a movement toward his father, but something in my face stops him. I can't believe he is going to help Croaker.

'What are you doing?' I ask, grabbing at him.

'There's no point,' Siôn says in a dead voice, not looking at me. 'He'll kill her anyway. Least I can stop her suffering so much.' He shrugs my arm off and goes to his father.

'What?'

'We sell them. For meat. It's time for her now.' He goes to Sky, his calm immediately soothing her. Her feet settle to the earth and her snorting subsides.

'No. No. Siôn!' I can't believe his betrayal. This is Siôn, he loves animals, he would never harm them. 'You can't kill her.' I go towards him, interrupting, putting myself between her and him.

He does not look at me, his gaze is lowered to his father.

'Will you tell that bitch to get out of it,' Croaker snarls, looking at Siôn not at me.

'Siôn! Come on,' I plead. I put myself between Siôn's arms, one either side of me as he holds Sky, his fingers taut in her mane.

He looks at me then, eyes brimming with hurt and fear. 'It will be quick. It's better this way.'

I see it. He can't say no to Croaker, he can't stand up to him, he can't find the strength to fight back. He doesn't know how.

But I have the strength. He has given it to me. There is no time to think.

It is less than a second. The time it takes for a punch or a slap. I am up on Sky's back. Siôn's grip slackens.

Croaker is mouthing silently and I see him raising his gun.

Siôn pushes his father's arm, the gun slips and the shot falls wide. The last thing I see is Croaker's fist meeting Siôn's temple with a crack as Sky gallops away for her life.

I cling to her neck, my thighs gripping and slipping and gripping again, as she sweats with desperation. My heart is galloping too, high and tight in my throat. I am doing this. I am. Not Siôn. Not Dad. Not Mum, but me.

I try to steer her to the wall where I remember the herd escaping to the moor, but she doesn't need me to tell her how to get away. She is bolting, over the wall and onto the moor. I have no idea what to do except to hang on. If I can keep going, find help, find Dad, maybe somehow I can save Sky.

CHAPTER TWENTY

I am terrified Croaker is behind us, that he will be on us in moments, to kill me for stealing his horse. My mind is fractured and loose, thoughts scattering and making no sense. I dare myself to look behind.

The mountain is there, as solid and unmoveable as always. Croaker and Siôn are nowhere to be seen on its great, dark back. I did it. I have rescued Sky.

The thrill subsides as I begin to get my breath back and look about.

The moor stretches out in front of us, an undulating, barren, beautiful space. The sun has set, and made the roof of the world a jungle of pinks and deepening darkness. The sky is so big, there is so much of it, blowing and wild, fighting with the grasses, tugging and grabbing, as though trying to tear the earth free of its roots. I wonder if Sky is as overwhelmed as me, as she stills herself, flanks heaving.

What now? There is no Siôn now to lead the way. Only me.

My hand feels cold, missing his touch, his warm, dry hand. A hand that kills?

He took that punch to save me, save Sky, didn't he?

I don't have any answers, only to keep going. I nudge Sky with my heels and she snorts quietly but complies, walking on.

There are no paths, only mile after mile of grassy space, mixed with dark boggy crevices that want to suck Sky's legs in and strand us in this dark. She is good though, picking her way carefully around the dangers, testing uncertain ground before she attempts to walk across. The one good thing about the gathering darkness is the occasional flash of a car headlight, far in the distance, that tells us the right direction to head. Keep going.

Dried tears have made hard runnels across my skin. If I am cold, I am too numb to know it. I can't feel my fingers, threaded tight in Sky's mane. She is still here. I am still here.

I wish Siôn was with us. My memory flashes with the crack of the punch, his beautiful body jolting backwards, the cower of his shoulders. Fresh tears seep over my cracked, dry skin.

I am not even angry that he lied. I can see why he never told me about the horses being killed. He's been escaping too: our secret den, our secret dream.

I have to keep reminding myself, I was the one who leaped on Sky's back and got her away from Croaker. If I can do that, I can work out how to get us to safety.

It is dark now. I clumsily dismount, deciding it's better if I go first, treading carefully, one exhausted step in front of the other.

This is Foulstone Moor. It was from Hagger Tor, up in the distance, that we scattered Mum's ashes. Those heavy handfuls of her that floated, dropped, scattered, across this dark expanse.

There is no moon, it's almost pitch-black dark, with the odd shape of land against sky; if it wasn't for our slow movement, I would wonder what was solid and what was air. My other senses are zinging with effort. I hear Sky's steady breathing next to my shoulder; occasionally her nose brushes me, the tickle of her mane on my cheek. I feel water soaking through my trainers each time I make a false move. The cold, high scent of the grasses, the constant buffeting of the wind. It would be easy to go mad up here.

A car zooms past on the road from Furneston, across the moors to Leeds, Yorkshire, beyond. It lights up the way. Not far now until we can put our feet on solid ground. Get home. And then–

I notice a quietness at my shoulder, a space.

'Sky? SKY?' I call. My voice sounds weak and tiny, strange in all the vastness. 'Sky?'

I turn, though it is hard to get any bearing at all. I panic, reaching out with my arms. No noise except the rustle of my clothes and the wind.

'SKY!' I cry. Sky. Sky. Where have you gone?

A neigh. Not far. I follow where I think the sound came from, and then my hands are against her thick neck, warm shoulder, tangled mane. My feet are sinking. I step back, my trainers shlooping as the bog tries to suck them in.

Sky neighs again. A tired sound. She isn't trying to move. I can hear her stillness.

I feel about my feet. The grass is relatively dry. I lie on my stomach and edge forward until I am at the start of the wet bog, the glue holding her. I can feel her two front legs. They're not in deep, only up to the first joint of her leg. I stand again.

'Come on, Sky, COME ON. I am NOT leaving you.' I feel in my pockets for any stray food. Nothing. 'Come on, we'll be home soon,' I try to coax. 'You can have lovely green grass in our garden. Come on, you're my girl now.'

She snorts.

'COME ON!' I shout at her. I lean across the bog. I butt at her with my head, like I've seen her do to the others to make them move. 'Come on, Sky.'

I can feel her trying to move, there is the shlooping sound as she manages to raise her foreleg.

'That's it. You can do it. Come to me. Here. Here.'

Her first leg misses and then she lands it on the solid ground next to my foot.

I shift. 'Good girl, again now.'

She is trying to move her back legs, but they must be in deeper.

'Try the other front one,' I say. 'COME ON!'

I push at her again, and she tries again. Her second leg hits solid ground.

'You can do it now, you can bring your weight to me.'

I feel her legs buckling and I think if she sits down we've had it.

'NO, SKY. Shhhusshhh now. Shhusshh. It's OK, it's OK. Here.' I try to pull at some of the grass at my feet. It's tough as wires, but she mouths at it anyway. I get some more. 'Right, let's try again.'

A car's lights wash over the moor. I get a brief glimpse of her; her back legs aren't in too deep, and the bog isn't too wide. Blackness again. I try to put my arms about her under her front legs. 'Come on now!'

I pull as hard as I can, my feet slipping on the wiry grass. I fall on my bottom as she uses her forelegs as leverage. There is a big 'shhhhhlooooop' and she is out, the momentum carrying her forward over me, mud falling from her across my head like rain. Her hoof almost lands on my stomach, but I roll to the side and she puts her weight down on the hard lovely ground.

'Well done, girl.' I lie staring into the darkness, enjoying the pure relief.

The belt of tarmac, hard and solid and real. Another car lights it up, and us. I wonder what the driver thinks, if she has seen us, ghosts on the edge of her vision, mud-covered and pale.

Sky tugs at the roadside grasses, as glad as me to be on solid ground. I know the way from here. I've been driven this way enough times. I know it's still a few miles till home.

Cars are passing occasionally, startling Sky with their glare and their noise. Her eyes are heavy and she is exhausted. I haven't the heart to ride her again. She takes some water from a brook that comes down into a pipe under the road. A road sign tells me Furneston is five miles further.

At last we reach the sulphur glow of the village lights up ahead, and the '30' sign. It is dead. The pub is shut up and there's no one on the street. I lead Sky up the lane, barely daring to breathe, anticipating the Land Rover, after everything.

The light is on in the lounge.

I lead Sky round to the back gate, unhook the catch and take her into the garden. The grass is long and Sky dips her head to graze wearily. I stroke her and put my forehead to her side. The back door is locked so I leave Sky, hooking the catch into place.

Dad is at the front door before I've even properly opened it, his frown lines etched deep.

'Kay, what the –?' He pushes his fist into his hair, then rubs his head. 'It's nearly one in the morning. I've been worried sick. Croaker was round earlier, says you've stolen his *horse*?'

Where do I start? I lean against the wall and close my eyes.

'I phoned the station and they've even had the patrol car out looking for you. Where have you been?'

I want Dad to simply know already, to take over and make it all right. 'Will you get me a bucket? I need some water. I've got the pony.' I gestured to my trainers, soaking and covered in mud.

'Here?'

'Yeah,' I sigh. 'Will you open the back door?'

He goes into the house, shaking his head, speechless.

After we've settled Sky as best we can, and I've dried off and had a sandwich and a cup of tea, Dad makes me explain. And I tell him, most of it, anyway.

'She can't go back there, Dad.'

'It's not illegal to shoot a horse, Kay. The pony's his property.'

'But Siôn says they'll sell her for meat. That's not right, is it? No one eats horse meat.'

'Well, it's not illegal to sell horses for the meat trade, Kay, even in our country.'

'But there's nothing wrong with her. She's wonderful. I can ride her easily, she's clever and strong.'

'Unfortunately, there are a lot of unwanted animals. If the farmers can make some money from it–' He trails off.

'I want her,' I say, looking at my socks. The assertive me is evaporating. I feel like a sulky child demanding a treat, but it is not that at all and I don't know how to make Dad see.

'Kay,' he admonishes softly.

'Well, why not? I can look after her. She really likes me and she is so easy.' I glare at him.

'You don't know anything about her health or history, do you? Where can we keep a pony? And you've got your exams…'

'You can't make me take her back.' I squeeze my fists into my eye sockets to stop the tears.

'I think we need to get some sleep. We will make a decision in the morning.' Dad rests his hands on his knees. 'Come on, you're shattered. We'll be able to think better after some sleep. OK? We won't decide anything until then.'

I keep my fists against my eyes, but the tears keep finding ways through the gaps. I don't even know how to put into words my fear for Siôn, for what might have happened, but I have to say something.

'And what about Siôn?' I look up.

'He's lived with his dad all his life. He's a grown man, Kay. I'm sure he can take care of himself.' A flicker in Dad's eyes. I know he doesn't quite believe that himself.

'But he can't. He is scared of Croaker, you should have seen him. He's like a child. He can't stand up to him.'

Dad bends down in front of me and puts his palms on mine.

'You think you know him, Kay, but–' He sees the hurt gathering in my eyes. 'The law can't do anything anyway.' He leans away. 'He's over sixteen and unless he wants to press charges for assault–'

I've had enough. The law. Dad always hides behind it. I have no strength left.

Dad stands up and takes my cup and plate, putting them in the kitchen, then he turns off the TV and waits for me to stand.

'Come on.' He hugs me.

I sleep fitfully. Siôn's face and his father's fist are on a loop in my brain; the high, panicked whinny of Sky; the barking mouth of Croaker. Every time I wake, the imprints of yesterday are in front of my eyes.

It's getting light when I wake again to a noise. I listen. But nothing, only Dad's snores in the other room. I need the toilet, so I drag my aching body out of bed. I open the frosted-glass window in the bathroom, to see Sky, before returning to my warm cocoon.

I can't see her in the rectangle of garden. The gate is still shut. She must be on the concrete patio. I can't see that from this window. I go down the stairs into the kitchen. She is not by the window.

I know of course that she has gone. But still I open the back door and go out in my bare feet to look.

There are hoof marks in the grass, semicircles and sickle moon shapes. The gate has been hooked back. Someone has taken her.

CHAPTER TWENTY-ONE

I can't see Dad, just a mound of duvet. His face is buried in the pillow. I never come in his bedroom. But I have to tell him. I shake the shape firmly.

'Dad.'

'It's not even six yet, Kay.'

'Sky's gone.'

Dad blinks the sleep away. He sees me, fully dressed, and sits up. 'You can't go up there, Kay. He's not safe.'

'Well, I am. You can't stop me.'

'Look, if you wait – I'll call a patrol car, I'll say we heard a disturbance.' Dad yawns.

But he doesn't. He goes into the bathroom. I hear the shower coming on. He is stalling. I slam the door when I leave, not caring about the neighbours.

There is no sign of anyone in the lane.

I jog up to the gate, then take the track down to the farm.

I can see the Land Rover. The curtains are half-pulled in the house and the front door is shut. There are two large stone outbuildings opposite; one of the big doors is open, but there's no sound. Even the dogs are quiet as I walk on, my stomach clenched, my breathing short.

I can see in at the kitchen window, where there's a collection of leads and rope on the sill and some cups. There is a crack in the pane above the front door, and the once-white wood is matted with black mud and spiders' webs.

Suddenly the dogs let rip a riot of barking. They are shut in behind a battered door in a second outbuilding – an old outside toilet or a stone toolshed. I can see their paws dancing behind the jagged slats as they roar and leap at the door to escape.

Croaker's heavyset frame looms out of the shadows of the open barn. He walks unhurriedly across the cobbles towards me, wiping his hands on his jeans.

I clear my throat. 'Is Sk – the pony here?'

'She's here.'

'Look, I'm sorry I took her. But, look, I'll pay you. I can take her off your hands and I'll give you the money you will get for selling her, more–'

He looks at me and I force myself to keep eye contact.

'You want her, do you?' he says, a half-grin on his fat face. I want to slap him. My heart is boom-booming in my ears.

'I'll look after her.' I know that's of no interest to him.

'Riding her off, hiding her at your copper's house. Thinking you can get the better of me.'

He stops a few centimetres from me. I can smell him: sour, old drink, old sweat. I can see the cross-weave of his khaki jumper. He's close. Too close.

'You women think you can all get the fucking better of me. But you can't.'

His ham-fingers grip my arm.

'Please,' I say, trying to pull my sleeve out of his grasp.

'And you're fucking our Siôn.'

He smiles at me and I know what that expression means. I've seen it before, a lustful flicker. Fear tightens my throat. I look round for Siôn.

'He's busy at the minute.' Croaker smiles. 'Come on, seeing as you're so interested. I'll give you a tour, and you can take the nag with you.'

He snickers to himself and tugs my arm. His grip is hard and tight, though he walks casually in the direction of the big barn. He can see me taking in the decay: the rotten wooden doors, the grass splitting the concrete, the broken glass in the windows.

'Fucking foot-and-mouth ruined us. They burned every one of my animals. How do they expect you to get over that?' He snorts and rubs his sleeve over his nose. If I can get him talking, maybe I can work out a way to get out of here.

'That's awful.' I try to sound sincere, but my hammering heart is making my words squeaky.

He sneers, and pulls me inside.

It's dark. I can see a dirty concrete floor and dark, unmoving shapes against the walls covered in black tarpaulin.

'There she is.' Croaker points to a shape on the floor, shrouded in the same thick material. Sticking out from the edge, are hooves. Still and silent.

I am rigid for a moment. Stunned. Then the horror of it registers.

'Bastard.' I throw my fist out at him. I try to punch him with my one free arm, Croaker, who killed Sky and hurt Siôn, but I am a useless fighter, and he laughs as he grabs hold of my other wrist, pinching them tight in his fists. I am shouting, screaming, fear pouring out of me, as I twist my hands. I kick.

But he is everywhere, using his torso, as he did

with Sky, cornering her, reining her in. He is pressing against me, his hot sour breath on my cheek, the spittle wetting my skin.

The car wheels squeak as they break and the doors bang. One, two patrol cars and Dad's crimson estate.

Croaker releases his grip and I fall to my knees in the mud and the dirt.

Dad is here. His warm fingers grip mine and haul me up, and his kind arms wrap around me and pull me out of that awful dark place. I look about me, blinking.

'Dad, where's Siôn? Where's Siôn?'

There are police in the barn, looking under the tarpaulins, opening up the other barn doors, letting the dogs out of their prison.

Croaker is in one of the cars, being questioned. His sly face glances out at me. Even sitting in the police car, he thinks he's got one over on me. What's he done?

'I'm sure he's fine. Probably still in bed, Kay.'

'No, no, he's not. That bastard's done something to him. He was so angry with him yesterday. He could have done anything. Killed him or anything.'

I run up to the house and bang on the door.

'Siôn, Siôn, it's me, open up!' I yell. 'Siôn!'

The door isn't locked. Inside the smell is foul. Damp, and rotting food. The carpet thick with grime. I turn the light on, but the low-watt bulb does little to the gloom.

'SIÔN!' I yell again. Dad stands behind me, his jacket crinkling. Apart from our breathing, there is no other sound.

I run up the stairs, trying not to touch anything as I climb. Dad's slower, heavier steps follow me.

There's a landing with a banister rail and three doors. The first to a dank empty bathroom; the second to a bedroom with a fusty double bed. A pile of clothes on the floor look like a body, and a scream rises in my throat, until Dad touches it with his foot. The pile collapses.

The third door leads to a smaller bedroom. It has a bed and an MDF wardrobe. The bed is made and the curtains open. Dad looks in astonishment at the skulls and scapula, fragments of feet and ribs that line the windowsill and decorate the top of the wardrobe.

'Siôn?' I call more quietly, my stomach dropping in dread.

'What is all this?' Dad touches the white shards with a finger.

'He collects them, from the mountain.'

Dad stares at me.

We walk back downstairs more slowly. There is a bare front room with a sofa and TV. In the kitchen, the dirty sink and few dishes give off a ripe odour.

'Siôn?'

I am beginning to wonder if he has gone to the den, escaped, when a door in the wall at the other end of the kitchen catches my eye.

'Dad.'

He goes to open it. It's locked. 'Siôn?' Dad calls, his face close to the door. He bangs hard and then puts his ear to the wood. 'I can hear something.'

He runs past me, calling the other officers in from outside. There's a lot of shouting and Dad and another officer ram the door. It won't budge, so they lift one of the kitchen benches and use that. On the third go, the door splinters around the lock and breaks, swinging open.

Steps lead down into a cellar. Someone calls for a torch, then finds the light switch.

Siôn is at the bottom of the steps. His face is swollen and his leg is twisted under him.

There's more talking and someone radios for an ambulance.

'Don't move him,' Dad calls as I squeeze past them and kneel by Siôn.

'Hey, it's me.'

His eyes stay closed but a smile tries to cross his face.

I smooth his crazy hair with my fingers. 'You're going to be OK now, Siôn. It's all going to be OK.' I clasp his cold hand in mine, taking care not to hurt him any further.

I cry as I look at him, his eyes moving under the skin of his eyelids, in some dream or nightmare. Then the paramedics arrive and bundle him into an ambulance.

'I've got to go with him,' I cry to Dad as I start to climb into the back of the van.

'You are in no fit state, Kay. Come home and get changed. We can go to the hospital then.' Dad takes both my hands and pulls me back out.

The doors are shut up and in the time it takes for me to breathe in and breathe out, the convoy of police and ambulance are driving off down the lane, past our house and beyond.

There is silence.

I am too numb to move or to think. The sun is up fully now, looking down on a bright summer's day. I see swallows flying their streamlined arcs above the barn, above the farmhouse. A white butterfly flickers through the sunlight and away.

'I've got to say goodbye to Sky.' My voice breaks as I stumble back to the dark cavern of the barn.

'No, Kay. Leave her.' Dad squeezes my hand and tries to turn me round, but I march ahead. In that hateful barn, I peel back the tarpaulin to look at my beautiful girl one last time.

A russet-coloured mane. Not white. Not snow-white, blossom-white, bone-white, Sky-white, but russet-red.

'Dad, Dad! It is not her!'

Both shouting, we scout through the farmyard, past the old toilet where the dogs were kept, through the gap between the barns, battling through the massive nettles almost as tall as me, that Dad has to kick out of the way with his boots, stamping them flat.

Past an ancient rusted tractor, surrounded by big empty tubs and knots of dirty polythene, we reach a corner of the farm the sun hasn't found yet; it hasn't pushed its warm fingers into Sky's soft coat, so I do it instead.

She is tethered to the back of the old tractor with a belt. I rip the belt away to get her free. She nuzzles in my pockets for polo mints, her warm wet breath on my fingers. I lean into her. I am crying. Her moving, living mane smells of the mountain.

CHAPTER TWENTY-TWO

I am desperate to see Siôn, but Dad won't let me. He makes me go home and take a bath and go to bed. I don't know how. Something about the way he talks leaves me no room to argue.

'Siôn is safe now, Kay. He is in the best place. We will go and see him later.' He runs me a bath and then shuts the bathroom door on me.

I begin to unzip and unbutton myself. I can see Sky's shape through the frosted glass in the back garden. No one will ever take her now.

There is dirt and blood on my hands. I turn them over, looking at the ridges of my knuckles, wondering if it is my blood or Siôn's. I don't know which. I feel washed out, outside and in, from all the crying, all the endings: of me and Siôn and our secret, of Mum and of losing who I was, that girl who believed in good things, that people you loved would get better, that

the time for treatment. It's the same smell, the same fake lighting, the same blankets with the little square holes in. The same heavy, dragging feeling back in my gut.

'He's only recently regained consciousness,' says the nurse, smiling over her specs at us. 'He hasn't said anything yet though.'

'Have the police said when they are coming to interview him?' Dad asks her.

She shakes her head. She goes to answer a phone, as we move down the corridor to Bay 2.

My stomach is knotting and knotting again.

Siôn is awake, though his eyes are closed. He opens the less bruised lid and looks at us. He's a mess: a cast on his leg, bandages round his bare chest, a massively swollen and cut face.

'Ouch,' I say, trying to smile at him, but he looks away from me out of the window. I see his Adam's apple moving as he swallows.

'Do you want a drink?' Dad gets a polystyrene cup and fills it with water. He holds the cup to Siôn's lips and he takes the tiniest sip.

'More?' Dad asks gently.

Siôn moves his head slightly to the side.

I root for Siôn's hand on the bed covers and give it a gentle squeeze. 'Hey, you.' I try to smile.

A tear slides out of his open eye, banks against his nose and drops to the pillow. Another follows. He blinks.

I close my eyes briefly. 'Does it hurt a lot?'

He tries to shrug, his gaze slipping away.

'Croaker's in custody and he won't get bail,' Dad says, 'so your mum could come.'

Siôn continues to look out of the window.

A nurse comes over. 'Don't worry, he'll mend.' She smiles cheerfully at me. I stand up to let her check his temperature.

'Is he eating?' Dad asks her, as she writes something on the chart at the foot of the bed.

'Not yet. It'd be good to drink something at least, Siôn.'

He turns to gaze at her, unfathomable.

'Have they told you when they'll be coming to interview him yet?' Dad asks again. The nurse goes off to check. 'I'll go and get some supplies from the shop. Chocolate, Siôn? Crisps?'

Siôn tries to shrug in reply. Dad looks at me but I have no idea either. So he goes off, happy to have something to do.

Siôn's eyes are leaking again, silently. 'I'm sorry,' he croaks.

'Don't.'

'About the ponies. I didn't want you to get too close. I couldn't stop him. I hated it.'

'I know.' I look at his face, the stinging tears ridging over his damaged face, the beautiful cheekbones obliterated by bruises. When I try to hug him, I can't smell Siôn at all, only the antiseptic, the blankness of the hospital.

'Did you get Sky away?' he asks, trying to shift forward a little, wincing and leaning back.

'She's safe. She's home with me.'

Siôn closes his eyes and tries a smile. 'I wish we were in the den now, me and you.'

I nod. 'Soon.'

I can see the dark uniforms of the police over in reception. I look at the rubble of Siôn's face.

'The police are here.'

Dad returns from the shop and stands around, chatting with them. I realise with a shock one of them is the woman who came to our house, it feels like months ago. What's her name? Sally? She has her hair up in a ponytail and is nodding as Dad speaks. They all three glance in our direction. Sally sees me and begins to smile. I look away.

'You've got to tell them the truth,' I say to Siôn as they walk over to the bed. 'Please. He isn't worth protecting.'

Siôn won't look at me again. Even when I kiss him goodbye.

CHAPTER TWENTY-THREE

'They managed to get hold of Siôn's mum,' Dad says, as he takes off his jacket and gives me a loose hug. This routine has started now – before leaving and returning, he gives me a little hug. I like it. It is a new thing for us both.

'What did she say?'

'She's coming. Tomorrow, if we can believe her.' He purses his lips.

'She will. I think she loves him. She's just scared.'

'If it was you, I wouldn't need any persuading.' He smiles at me.

'If you were Siôn's dad, he wouldn't be in this mess.'

I feel glad right then: at least I have a dad – a good man, one who knows right from wrong and lets me be me.

I can't wait to tell Siôn when we visit later. He'll

be pleased, though I doubt he'll admit it. He is impossible to read sometimes. He's been in four days now and is getting better. The bruising is going down and he can move more, but he is like a plant out of the sun stuck in the hospital. He needs to go home.

I watch the rain make glassy rivulets on the window. I notice then, for the first time since we moved to Blackmoss Lane, how I want to be here, in the safe and in the warm, while Dad tinkers about in the rest of the house. It feels like there is a space again, not full of –? What has it been full of? I guess I have been angry. Just so angry.

'Can we decorate, Dad?' I follow him into the kitchen, where he has set his bike upside down, constantly fiddling with the cog and chain. He looks round the kitchen as though for the first time.

'It is a bit gloomy, this old paper, isn't it?'

'Er, a bit,' I say, rolling my eyes.

'We could go to PaintnRoll at the weekend, if you like?'

'OK. I'll take this stuff upstairs.' I lift the pile of washing off the kitchen counter. It still feels like I am doing Mum's job. But I put that from my mind. The clothes billow up to my chin.

Dad smiles, his eyebrows slightly raised.

I put my own stuff away first, properly: the

underwear in the drawers, smoothing my T-shirts down as I fold them and put them away, instead of the usual scrunching and forcing them in wherever I can.

The rest is towels and spare bedding. Where would Mum put them? Towels go in the airing cupboard, but there isn't enough room for the bedding too.

I am OK with this job. It's almost as though things are normal. Mum is out and I am helping, wanting to impress her when she gets back.

The big wardrobe in Dad's room still looks empty with only Dad's boring black, white and grey clothes hanging in there. It looks gaping and hungry without Mum's clothes to share it. There are shelves along one side, with the odd box and bag that never got unpacked when we moved. I put them together onto one shelf, to leave the other one clear for the bedding.

As I lift up one of the Sainsbury's bags, I glance inside. A glimpse of soft brown leather, and a faint smell of her.

I sit on the edge of Dad's bed and take it out. Mum's handbag.

Time stops.

It smells of her, make-up and polos.

I unzip the central compartment. Her purse is

inside. A USB cable. A few bits of paper. I flick through them. An outpatient's card from the hospital. A newspaper cutting about the benefits of acupuncture for cancer patients. A photo of me and Dad on the beach in Cyprus last year. A list of things to tell the doctor: symptoms, dizzy spells, dates and times.

The light is gloomy. I can hear Radio 2 downstairs and Dad humming along.

I am teetering on the edge of that great empty space inside me, about to dive in. I slip down to the floor, tucking my knees up tight, and keep looking.

Her car keys, to the car sold months ago. I feel the weight of them in my hand, remember sitting next to her in the front seat singing to some Oasis tune, her hair blowing out and touching my face.

A creased handkerchief. Some Milk of Magnesia tablets. Her blue hair bobble, wound round the handle of her brush, her soft brown hair twisted in between the spikes. I pick a little at the hair, smoothing it out. It still smells of shampoo and Mum. There's the little felt owl I gave her for good luck when she went for treatment; a scrunched up receipt for petrol; a card sending Mum love, love, love. The debris of her life, when she was moving and living and talking and loving, her body still working, breathing and being.

'Do you want some tea, Kay?' Dad stops at the door.

I turn my face so he can't see the tears. He stands for a moment, taking in Mum's bag, all the things scattered round me like fallen leaves.

'Kay?'

'Go away.' I don't want him to put this into words; because it means admitting it, the raw blank plain truth of her, dead and gone. Putting it into words – making it something we can manage, we can name and explain, and one day get over and move beyond.

But he does not leave.

'It's all right to cry, you know.' His voice is full with emotion, but I've no space for his feelings. I am bursting with my own.

I shake my head, the tears raging silently, wetting my hair and T-shirt.

'Talk to me, Kay.' He kneels by the door.

'How?' I snarl, turning to him at last. 'How can I talk about this –?' and I hit my chest. 'There's no words for this.'

I hit myself again, my teeth clenched. Dad tries to come to me, to close his arms around me, contain me, but I shriek, 'And you, you gave her things away! You took her away from me, her things, her things!'

217

'Kay, love, they're only things. They won't bring her back.'

I hold my stomach, kneeling over, mewing like an animal, and snarl, 'I KNOW. Now this is all that's left.'

I throw the dry bits of paper up into the air. Dad's face is lined with tears as he watches me. And I know he still loves her; he loves me too.

'How can she be gone? Why couldn't they save her?' How can this be all that is left of the person who filled my life and bossed me and tended me and minded me and grew me and loved me best of all – an old bag?

And the rage – at last it peaks and bursts through. The grief and sorrow flood the room and the approaching twilight, and I let Dad hold me then, not like Mum would have done, snugged up in her softness, but like Dad, in a rumpled, awkward, sideways hug. And he says, 'You cry, love. You cry.'

SUMMER

It has been weeks. I don't how to explain it really, but something has shifted inside of me, the way morning sunlight flickering in through the kitchen window can make the difference between a good morning and a bad one.

After all the drama, it was hard to place myself back in my life. Dad agreed I didn't have to go to school, apart from exams. He insisted I went and sat every one, though I'd done no revising and will probably fail them all. I saw Anna there, but there was never time to chat, and to be honest I didn't want to. She's started to smile at me, raising her eyes occasionally after a difficult paper, as we all filed out of the exam hall.

The long summer stretches out in front of me. I've got an interview for a course that starts in September, but I don't know what they will think of my results when they come in. Dad has been really good about it. He says, 'You've got to keep it in perspective. Look at what you've been through this year.'

It helps having Sky in my life. I have to get up to feed her, and muck her out. She's got her own little field now down the lane, with a shelter when the weather's bad. We're going to buy a proper saddle when Dad gets paid.

The doorbell rings and I roll off the bed. It sounds weird. Not many people come round here since we moved. I never invited anyone. But I know who this is.

Dad invites Anna into the hall, saying some cringy dad-type joke. She is smiling. Then she sees me and she smiles at me.

I'd forgotten Dad always thought he was funny.

We go through into the garden and sit on the deckchairs. The sun is hot and the air still.

'You OK?' she asks, squinting in the sun, her hand shielding her eyes so she can look at me properly.

'Good days, bad days.' I smile.

'I got you this.' She hands me a gift bag with a blue bear on it. Inside is a red heart-shaped box. I take it out and open the lid. She's given me a white piece of card with a four-leaf clover taped on it.

'Is this the one you found...?'

'...years ago. Yeah, do you remember, on the rough field? You were gutted cos you couldn't find one.'

I turn it over in my fingers. There's a silence between us, a rest or a pause. My breath comes and goes. The bottle of my body fills.

'It's for good luck. For your interview. Don't cry,' she says.

'Happy tears,' I laugh. 'Thank you.'

And I am grateful, truly grateful, to see Anna again, simply to sit with her and feel the sun on our faces. I knit my fingers together, push my hands out and up, stretch my arms and feel the cogs in my spine elongate, shuffle and sigh with pleasure.

'I'm sorry, Kay, about bailing out on you,' Anna says, her hand shielding her eyes, trying to read my expression.

'Don't,' I say. 'It was my fault.'

'No. No, it wasn't. I was just – well. It doesn't matter now. We've split up, me and Joe. Jess saw him cheating on me last month, so that's it. All over.'

'Are you all right?'

It's her turn to well up, closing her eyes to the sun. I reach across and hug her. She reciprocates, but it is over quickly. And I am left thinking how everyone has their limits, even best friends. And she is still my friend, but.

'God, look at me,' she says, wiping her face. 'Sorry. Come on, tell me everything that's been happening with you.'

So I do. I tell her first about my beautiful Sky, then all about Croaker, and all about Siôn. I feel myself full of story again, my own story.

I tell her how Siôn's leg has mended fine and he's home at Hagg Farm with his mum, though how long she will stay for, nobody knows; how Croaker's got his court date, but still hasn't had his trial yet. Dad thinks he'll get about five years for it, all in all, now Siôn has admitted it was Croaker who threw him down the cellar and left him there.

'I don't get it though, because Siôn wants to visit him in prison, and if my dad had done that to me I'd never want to see him again.'

Anna shrugs. 'Well, he did look a bit – weird.'

'What?' I sit up. 'When did you see him?'

'That day on the train. Remember? Lots of crazy hair.'

'Oh yeah.' I lie back in the sun, remembering the buzz I felt just seeing him. 'He is a bit weird. But–'

'Suits you well then.'

'Oy, Anna Twonk!'

Some days I don't think of her much at all, but Mum is in my mind a lot today. I have her voice in my head when I am getting ready. *Kay, why do you always leave everything till the last minute?*

I am thinking about it while I get dressed. I know now there's no time limit on grieving. I thought, you know, a year of grieving and then I'd be back to 'normal'. Except there is no going back, because grief moves you on, somewhere strange and new. It is more like seasons, I think, the way it comes and goes; sometimes I still wake up crippled by it, but now at last I can let myself cry, and then it's easier to get up, get on.

Dad offers to drive me in, but I want to do it on my own. I'm not being mean, it's only, you know, growing up, I guess.

I am so nervous waiting my turn to be interviewed; those little tummy flies giving me grief. Another girl comes out, smiles at me. I like her shoes. It is my turn. They talk about the course and ask me questions about my predicted grades and then one of them mentions my *recent personal circumstances*. I have to say it out loud: 'My mum died of cancer in January.'

It's weird to see the effect of those few words. There is a pause, then the woman says, 'That must have been very hard for you.' And for the first time I don't want to roar at her.

I say, 'It is. Yes.' They move on.

Anyway, they said they can't confirm a place until the results are in, but are *highly impressed by the comments from my teachers* and something about mitigating circumstances. So we'll see. I've done all I can for now.

The sun is out.

I like town. I like how full it is. It's a buzz here, everything moving, so many people. So different from Blackmoss Lane. I am wondering whether to get a bus, when I realise the tramp standing next to me is peeing in the bush. He is right next to the main road, with so many people passing. He reminds me of Croaker, his shape, his build. I shudder as I move away. I am not ready for compassion for Croaker quite yet.

I decide to walk. Out up the main street, skittling up a pavement that is bigger than our lane. It is filled with students, bags over their shoulders, music on, or in pairs, threes, sometimes more. I nip through, slipping and darting. I can feel my legs working, the bones in my feet balancing in my shoes against this hard ground, my toes springing me onwards.

I turn off the main road, down Milk Street.

Someone has stuck a pink cartoon cow on the street sign. I check the time, then take a seat on the bench, next to an old couple whose bag scratches my leg as they get up to leave.

I am outside Marks and Spencers; near the enormous metal wind sculptures, by the steps; I am one of the throng of people, in their strappy tops and sunglasses, or sweltering in suits because it's the kind of day you might not quite gauge the weather properly, or maybe this is England at its finest.

There are stripy jumpers and full skirts, yellow shirts and pleated trousers; a small stubborn boy pulled to attention by his father, a balloon bobbing with the tug of an arm; a line of young silver birch, with their slim limbs and nest of green, just beginning; there is a warm breeze touching and connecting everything I can see.

And in the breeze is a sea of invisible dust, particles of plants and spiders' legs, of pony hair and dog fur, skin cells and fashion, carbon and salt and vinegar crisps, of sulphur, carcinogens and pollen, gold and feathers, brick and sand, of glass and of me too.

There is the rumble of buses, the rustle of bags and I am thinking about Mum again.

She is dead, but I am alive and I am relieved and

lost and happy and sad all together, and those feelings too float away, like dust, and are caught by the same warm breeze that is rippling the blue of a shirt. The shirt suggests his shape, and billows out again.

His eyes are on the ground. There is his lope, the swing of his limbs. There is the pause in my breath when he glances up at me and smiles. I walk towards him.

ACKNOWLEDGEMENTS

First of all thank YOU for caring enough about my book to even read the acknowledgements!

If I didn't have my band of good friends cheering me on from the sidelines, I would have never finished this book, let alone undertaken the journey to get it published. Thank you to Emma Walton, for reading early drafts and being utterly chive-alicious; to Ruth, the Edwards and Hodson clan, for their warmth and support over many many years; to Pandora Lapington for being my first YA reader, and for wanting more! And a very special thank you to Liz Challinor for her untiring belief in my creativity, and reminding me of the way when I was lost.

Thanks to all my family, near and far. To Pete for keeping me fed, grounded and in the real world! To my children, Dylan and Rose for liking my stories, and being the reason for it all. To my Dad for so much: oak trees and tea and kind, quiet space and filaments and motes and words. To my Mum for the unceasing and unconditional love that powers me.

Thanks to Janet, Meg and all at Firefly for having the courage to publish this story with sex, alcohol and swearing in it! To Izzy Ashford for the cover design. To Bangor Cellar Writing Group for friendship, warmth and wit, and reminding me I can write. To SCBWI BI, especially the North Wales troop, for enthusiasm and camaraderie. To my brilliant students who make me laugh – keep reading!

Lastly, thanks to Literature Wales for their excellent critiquing service that gave me hope.

If anyone has been affected by the issues in this book, please contact CRUSE who offer bereavement support for young people: www.cruse.org.uk. There is also MIND who can help with mental health issues, such as depression: www.mind.org.uk.